Cliffs

MW01697456

ON BRADBURY'S

FAHRENHEIT 451

by Kristi Hiner

IN THIS BOOK!

- Get the author background and literary context you need to fully understand the book
- Learn the important traits and motivations of all the major characters
- Know what happens *and* what it means with detailed Summary & Analysis
- Deepen your knowledge with Critical Essays covering key aspects of the book
- Check your understanding with study help and review questions

LEARNEO

CliffsNotes® On Bradbury's *Fahrenheit 451*
Published by:
Learneo, Inc.
2000 Seaport Blvd., Third Floor
Redwood City, CA 94063
www.learneo.com

Cataloging-in-Publication information is available from the Library of Congress.
ISBN-13: 978-1-957671-81-9

Table of Contents

INTRODUCTION AND CONTEXT

Book Summary

Set in the twenty-fourth century, *Fahrenheit 451* introduces a new world in which control of the masses by the media, overpopulation, and censorship has taken over the general population. The individual is not accepted and the intellectual is considered an outlaw. Television has replaced the common perception of family. The fireman is now seen as a flamethrower, a destroyer of books rather than an insurance against fire. Books are considered evil because they make people question and think. The people live in a world with no reminders of history or appreciation of the past; the population receives the present from television.

Ray Bradbury introduces this new world through the character Guy Montag, the protagonist, during a short time in his life.

The story begins with an inciting incident in which Montag meets Clarisse McClellan. Montag, a fireman who destroys books for a living, is walking home from work one day when the young Clarisse approaches him and introduces herself. Clarisse is the antithesis of anyone Montag has ever met. She is young, pretty, and energetic, but more importantly, she converses with him about things that he has never considered. Her inquisitive nature fascinates him because she ponders things such as happiness, love, and, more importantly, the contents of the books that he burns.

At first, Montag tries to ignore her questions, but on the rest of his walk home, he cannot get the young girl out of his mind. Upon entering his home, however, her image is quickly erased. Montag enters his bedroom to find an empty bottle of sleeping pills lying on the floor next to his bed. He discovers that his wife Mildred (Millie), whether intentionally or unintentionally, has overdosed on the pills. He calls the emergency squad, and the strangers come with their machine to save his wife.

The next morning, Montag attempts to discuss what happened the night before, but his wife is uninterested in any type of discussion. She avoids Montag's questions and instead focuses on the new script she has received for an interactive television program. Montag, though frustrated and confused about what happened the previous night, heads off to work.

On his way to work, Montag again encounters Clarisse and is left pondering things like the taste of rain and what dandelions represent.

He enters the fire station and immediately encounters the Mechanical Hound, who actually growls at him. Because of this brief encounter, Montag realizes that the Hound doesn't like him, a point that he quickly points out to his fellow fireman, Captain Beatty.

Several days pass since Montag's last meeting with Clarisse. During one of his final conversations with Clarisse, Montag learns that she fears the violence in her peers. She points out that their world used to be an entirely different world, one where pictures showed actual people and people talked about important things.

One day at the fire station, the firemen receive a call that an old woman has stashed books in her house. The firemen race to her home and begin destroying the contraband. Montag urges the woman to leave the house because the entire home will be destroyed, but she refuses to leave her precious books. The home, along with the old woman and her books, is set aflame, but not before Montag steals one of the books.

Later the same night, Montag tries to discuss the day with Millie, but she is not interested in what he has to say. During their conversation, Montag discovers from Millie that Clarisse was killed in an automobile accident.

Montag decides to call in sick to work the next day, but he is surprised by a visit from Beatty. Somehow, Beatty knows that Montag is keeping a book, and he is interested in reading it. Beatty converses at great length with Montag and tells him that every fireman gets the itch to read a book at some point in his career. Beatty also tells Montag that even though he may keep the book for twenty-four hours, he must return to work, with book in hand, so the book can be properly destroyed.

After this meeting, Montag shows Millie that he has been hiding, not just one book, but a cache of books in the house for some time. He then convinces Millie to sit and read the books with him. While reading, Montag attempts to converse with Millie about the content of the books but finds that she cannot comprehend, nor does she want to comprehend, what they are reading.

At this point, Montag remembers an old, retired English professor, Faber, whom he had met in a park. Montag decides to visit Faber to gain more understanding about books and his recurrent thoughts.

Upon reaching Faber's house, Montag is first greeted by the old man with fear. Faber worries that Montag has come to burn his books and home, but he is quickly pacified when he sees Montag's Bible and hears that Montag wants to talk with him. During their conversation, Faber agrees to teach Montag, and he gives Montag a seashell radio so they can communicate with one another.

Montag returns home to find Mrs. Phelps and Mrs. Bowles, two of Millie's friends, at his home. Feeling especially courageous, Montag decides to enlighten them by reading "Dover Beach," but instead, he causes problems for himself because he scares the women. They flee the house in tears, and Millie is angry with him for causing the scene.

With Faber still speaking in his ear, Montag returns to work and gives Beatty a book, which is promptly incinerated. After a lengthy discussion with Beatty, an alarm comes into the station, and the firemen rush to destroy the next house. When the firemen stop in front of the unfortunate house, Montag is surprised to see his own home.

Promptly, Beatty orders Montag to destroy his home and places him under arrest. Montag takes a perverse pleasure in destroying the home, especially the television, and in the following moments, he also kills Beatty with his flamethrower. The Mechanical Hound attacks Montag before he can escape, but he destroys it with fire before the Hound can destroy him.

Montag runs to Faber's home for protection but quickly realizes that he is endangering Faber. Thus, he stops at the home of Black, a fellow fireman, and hides the books inside the house to incriminate him. Montag then reaches Faber's home, and Faber tells him to escape down the river because another Mechanical Hound is on the search for him.

After helping Faber rid all trace of him, Montag races toward the river in hopes of escaping the search. By the time the Mechanical Hound reaches the river, Montag's trail is lost. He safely floats down the river toward a group of social outcasts and criminals like himself.

Montag leaves the river and immediately finds the group that Faber told him about. He meets the unacknowledged leader of the group, Granger, who welcomes Montag to join them. Although he thought that the search was called off, Montag finds out that it was just rerouted. He watches on television as an innocent man, strolling along the city streets, is purposefully identified as Montag and is killed for the entire television audience to see.

The group decides to move on from their current site, and while they are walking, Granger explains the purpose of the outlaw group: They are preserving books by memorizing their contents and then destroying them. Books can not be forgotten, because each person in the group is a living version of them. Montag becomes the Book of Ecclesiastes from the Bible.

As the men continue in their journey, Montag and Granger watch as bombs fall upon the city and destroy everything in their path. The final war has begun. Although the men are escaping the city, they decide, without discussion, to return to the city with Montag in the lead.

About *Fahrenheit 451*

Introduction

Critics find Bradbury's most interesting years the post-World War II years, 1947-57, a period that roughly corresponds to a time when science fiction authors began to approach their subject matter seriously and were creating characters who had psychological complexity and ambiguity. During this decade, Bradbury produced some of his most vital works: *Dark Carnival* (Arkham House, 1947); the amazing *Martian Chronicles*(Doubleday, 1950), his first and perhaps finest science fiction work; the short story collections *The Illustrated Man* (Doubleday, 1951) and *The Golden Apples of the Sun* (Doubleday, 1953); and *Dandelion Wine*(Doubleday, 1957), a short novel that has attained the status of being a minor American classic.

During this period, Bradbury also produced "The Fireman," a short story that appeared in the second issue of *Galaxy Science Fiction* (February 1951) and was expanded into *Fahrenheit 451* (October 1953), his best and best-known novel. Initially published by Ballantine with two other stories, "The Playground" and "And the Rock Cried Out," *Fahrenheit 451* was not published separately until the Ballantine paperback release in April 1960.

Major Theme of *Fahrenheit 451*

Interestingly, the impetus for the characters and the situation of *Fahrenheit 451* date earlier than "The Fireman." They first appeared during the years immediately following World War II, as Bradbury reveals in his introduction to *Pillar of Fire and Other Plays* (Bantam, 1975):

This story ["Pillar of Fire," *Planet Stories*, Summer 1948], this character . . . I see now were rehearsals for my later novel and film *Fahrenheit 451*. If Montag is a burner of books who wakens to reading and becomes obsessed with saving mind-as-printed-upon-matter, then Lantry [protagonist of "Pillar of Fire"] is the books themselves, he is the thing to be saved. In an ideal world, he and Montag would have met, set up shop, and lived happily ever after: library and saver of libraries, book and reader, idea and flesh to preserve the idea.

By Bradbury's own admission, the thematic obsession that explicitly emerges in *Fahrenheit 451* is the burning of books, the destruction of mind-as-printed-upon-matter. And although Bradbury never uses the word "censorship" in the novel, one should be aware that he is deeply concerned with censorship. Book burning is a hyperbolic phrase that describes the suppression of writing, but the real issue of the novel is censorship.

If "Pillar of Fire" is read sensitively, one finds that not all books are in danger in the future *dystopia* (an imaginary world where people lead dehumanized, fearful lives), but particular kinds, or genres, of books are at risk. This theme, of course, is not precisely true of *Fahrenheit 451* in which all books that are burned by the "firemen" are in danger. This novel may be understood as a kind of hyperbolic extension of the tensions of the earlier story.

Bradbury's observation about "Pillar of Fire" (1948) begs the questions: What are the social and/or economic forces that caused such a thematic obsession to emerge in Bradbury's work from the period 1948-53? Why are only books of imagination, fantasy, and the macabre and occult threatened in "Pillar of Fire"?

Works by fantasists are also threatened in Bradbury's story "Usher II" (1950), which appears in *The Martian Chronicles* (1950). "Pillar of Fire" thus becomes a rehearsal for the themes of "Usher II," and the latter story appears to inhabit the same imaginative realm as does "The Firemen" published in 1951. ("The Firemen" was written during the same period as "Usher II" and is copyrighted 1950.) Indeed, the character of William Lantry in "Pillar of Fire" and the character of William Stendahl in "Usher II" are quite similar, as are the authors whose books are threatened — Poe, Bierce, and other American fantasists. Moreover, a Burning Crew is referred to in "Usher II," one that eventually burns Stendahl's beloved library of imaginative literature, and the Burning Crew is obviously a synonym for the firemen in *Fahrenheit 451.*

The question may be asked in another way: Why is Bradbury sensitive to the popular condemnation of fantasy literature? By extension, this question becomes an issue of the literary merit of works of popular literature. Why is Bradbury particularly sensitive to the critical reception of fantasy literature during the post-World War II period? The question becomes even more problematic when one considers that Bradbury himself was publishing science fiction and fantasy in legitimate magazines, or *slicks*, such as *Colliers* and the *Saturday Evening Post*, not in the *pulps*, or disreputable magazines. As Peter Nicholls observes, "[Bradbury's] career remains the biggest breakthrough into lush markets made by any genre of writer" (1985).

Genre Science Fiction

Far from traditional literary discussion, the questions posed may offer another way of reading the novel — as genre science fiction. After all, Bradbury's obsessions with the suppression of fantasy literature may express, at the psychological level, the wrestling with the validity of his own career as a fantasist. *Fahrenheit 451* represents Bradbury's first published novel, written at a time when — according to Brian W. Aldiss (Schocken, 1974) — "science fiction was still a minority cult, little known to any but its devotees." In his brief authorial statement appended to the beginning of *The October Country* (Ballantine, 1955), an abridgement of his earlier collection *Dark Carnival* (1947), Bradbury feels compelled to tell his readers that "[This book] will present a side of my writing that is probably unfamiliar to them, and a type of story that I rarely have done since 1948." By 1955 (during a time when his earliest work was out-of-print), Bradbury was aware of his (perhaps undeserved) reputation as a science fiction writer and was attempting to present to his readership an aspect of his work with which they were unfamiliar. Unsurprisingly, his next published book after *The October Country*, *Dandelion Wine* (Doubleday, 1957), is not science fiction, but a tour de force of juvenalia — specifically, a celebration of adolescence and the life-affirming value of the imagination. With the exception of *A Medicine for Melancholy* (Doubleday, 1959), a collection of short stories dominated by science fiction selections, Bradbury has rarely returned to science fiction. (Collections such as *R is for Rocket* [1962] and *S is for Space* [1966] only recycle earlier stories.)

But another aspect of *Fahrenheit 451* is equally interesting: The suppression and condemnation of imaginative literature (viewed earlier as synecdoche for popular literature) represent the development of an increasingly oppressive political organization that wishes to deny originality and idiosyncrasy. *Fahrenheit 451* uses the science fiction motif of *dystopia* — a totalitarian, highly centralized, and, therefore, oppressive social organization that sacrifices individual expression for the sake of efficiency and social harmony, all of which are achieved through technocratic means. The reader may examine the episodes of *Dandelion Wine* — the book most contiguous with *Fahrenheit 451* (disregarding *The October Country*) — originally published as "The Happiness Machine" and "The Trolley" (*Good Housekeeping*, Vol. 141 No. 1, July 1955.). The former story views technology as unable to provide for — and as even opposed to — human happiness; the latter story views technological innovation as solely efficient, as oppressive, and, perhaps, as even protofascist. In fact, one may find that *Dandelion Wine*, published after Bradbury became labeled as a formidable science fiction writer, views technology and technological innovation as inconsequential in solving basic human problems. This view is apparent in *Fahrenheit 451*. For example, note the marital problems between Montag and his wife — even though their home is full of technological contrivances specifically designed for domestic bliss — or explore the motivation for the development of the Mechanical Hound as a vehicle of social control via terrorist means.

Historical Influences for *Fahrenheit 451*

Despite all the rich possibilities of exploration in *Fahrenheit 451*, the issue of book burning, or censorship, remains most central to the novel and is the most difficult issue with which to grapple. In essence, book burning is synonymous with irrationality in the twentieth century. The genesis of *Fahrenheit 451* was presumably contagious with the period of Nazi anti-intellectualism during the late 1930s, and book burning certainly became a synonym for anti-intellectualism in science fiction of the 1950s — as it was in Walter M. Miller's *A Canticle for Leibowitz* (Lippincott, 1959). *Fahrenheit 451* emerged during a period of extreme interest in what Brian W. Aldiss calls "an authoritarian society" that roughly corresponds to the years 1945-1953, as revealed in George Orwell's *Animal Farm* (1945) and *1984* (1948); B.F. Skinner's *Walden Two* (1948); Kurt Vonnegut's *Player Piano* (1952); Evelyn Waugh's *Love Among the Ruins* (1953); and Frederick Pohl and C.M. Kornbluth's *The Space Merchants* (1953). Moreover, the postwar period also produced several novels and films concerned with the possibilities of nuclear holocaust, which hovers over Montag's world throughout the novel.

The novel also appears during the era known as the McCarthy period, the postwar political climate characterized by xenophobia, blacklisting, and censorship. In June 1949, for example, Representative John S. Wood asked some seventy colleges to submit their textbooks for examination and approval by the Un-American Activities Committee. Bradbury himself (*Nation*, May 2, 1953), in an article on science fiction as social criticism, suggested that "when the wind is right, a faint odor of kerosene is exhaled from Senator McCarthy." Many of the issues explored in the novel cannot be separated from the historical period in which they appeared. This assertion is not to say, however, that they are no longer relevant or timely issues. Indeed, the novel evidently held a particular fascination for readers in the 1980s when censorship in schools and libraries resurged. Although the novel initially went through six printings in its first twelve years (1953-1965), it went through twenty printings in the next five years (1966-1971) and has been in print since its initial publication.

As stated earlier, *Fahrenheit 451* is Bradbury's best-known novel, which, incidentally, happens to be science fiction. The novel need not, nor should it be, read only by science fiction or fantasy enthusiasts. *Fahrenheit 451* is, among other things, a genuine cultural document of the early 1950s as well as a book of great imagination — regardless of its genre.

Character List

Guy Montag The protagonist, an unhappy, complacent man who is thirty years old. He has been a fireman for ten years. He meets Clarisse and finds that her outlook on life is refreshing.

Mildred Montag (Millie) Guy's self-destructive wife, also thirty years old, who reveals to Montag the alienated existence of citizens in his society. She has never wanted children and considers her family to be television characters.

Clarisse McClellan Montag's new neighbor, seventeen years old, who calls herself crazy and enjoys conversations. Her recalcitrance and nonconformity allow Montag to discover how jaded his view of life has become.

Captain Beatty The antagonist of the book and Montag's superior, the Fire Captain, who functions as the apologist for the dystopian culture in which Montag lives. He is well read and uses his knowledge of books as a weapon to fight curiosity about them.

Mechanical Hound A machine, similar to a trained killer dog that the firefighters use to track down and capture criminals. The Hound disables and kills offenders with a morphine or procaine needle.

Unidentified Woman A woman from the ancient part of the city. Her martyrdom reveals to Montag the power of civil disobedience, books, and ideas.

Faber An elderly man, a retired English professor who is an underground, though ineffectual, scholar. He becomes Montag's ally and mentor.

Granger An ex-writer who is the unacknowledged leader of the social outcasts and criminals. He unites the group to keep the content of books safe.

Stoneman and Black Montag's fellow firemen who are conformists, and conservatives. Together with Beatty, they form Montag's familiar working colleagues.

Mrs. Phelps and Mrs. Bowles Millie's friends who do not question the social structure. Their husbands are called away to war. They also view the television characters as their families and become agitated when Montag reads to them.

Fred Clement, Dr. Simmons, Professor West, Reverend Padover, and Harris in Youngstown Social outcasts and criminals who are led by Granger. They choose and memorize a book to ensure that the story is never forgotten.

Ray Bradbury Biography

Personal Background

American novelist, short-story writer, essayist, playwright, screenwriter, and poet — Ray Bradbury was born in Waukegan, Illinois on August 22, 1920, the third son of Leonard Spaulding Bradbury and Esther Marie Moberg Bradbury. Often said to be America's best science fiction writer, Bradbury has also earned acclaim in the fields of poetry, drama, and screenwriting. As a young boy, Bradbury's life revolved around magic, magicians, circuses, and other such fantasies. Whenever traveling circuses pitched their tents in Waukegan, Bradbury and his brother were always on hand. Blackstone the Magician came to town when Bradbury was eleven, and he attended every performance. Mr. Electrico, another magician of sorts, particularly impressed Bradbury with his death-defying electric chair act. In fact, this magician once gave young Bradbury such a convincing talk that Bradbury decided to become a magician — the best in the world!

Bradbury's love of fantasy was encouraged by his family. Their favorite time of the year was Halloween, which they celebrated with even more enthusiasm than they celebrated Christmas. When Bradbury was eight, his Aunt Neva helped him devise the grandest Halloween party imaginable. The Bradbury home was transformed into a haunted house with grinning pumpkins, ghost-like sheets hanging in the cellar, and raw chicken meat representing parts of a dead witch. In years to come, these details furnished material for Bradbury's stories.

In addition to Bradbury's magician heroes, Buck Rogers, Flash Gordon, and Tarzan ranked high on his list of favorites. Bradbury read the series of books about the Emerald City of Oz, and his Aunt Neva read him the terror-filled tales of Poe. All these stories with their fantastic characters and settings were dramatic influences on Bradbury's later life.

Literary Career

Bradbury began his writing career in 1931 at age eleven, using butcher paper that he had to unroll as his story progressed. The following year, he and his family moved from Illinois to Arizona, and that same year, Bradbury received a toy typewriter on which he wrote his first stories.

In 1934, when he was fourteen, his family moved from Arizona to Los Angeles, where his writing career began to solidify. In 1937, he became a member of the Los Angeles Science Fiction League, whose help enabled him to publish four issues of his own science-fiction fan magazine, or "fanzine," *Futuria Fantasia*. Bradbury's graduation from a Los Angeles high school in 1938 ended his formal education, but he furthered it himself — at night in the library and by day at his typewriter. His first professional sale was for a short story entitled "Pendulum," co-authored with Henry Hasse; it appeared in *Super Science Stories*, August 1941, on Bradbury's twenty-first birthday. In 1942, Bradbury wrote "The Lake," the story in which he discovered his distinctive writing style. By 1943, he had given up his job selling newspapers and began writing full time, contributing numerous short stories to periodicals. His short story "The Big Black and White Game" was selected for Best American Short Stories in 1945.

Bradbury married Marguerite McClure in 1947, and the same year, he gathered much of his best materials and published them as *Dark Carnival*, his first short story collection. From then on, Bradbury's fantasy works were published in numerous magazines throughout the country.

Bradbury says that he learned to write by recalling his own experiences. Many of his early stories are based, unsurprisingly, on his childhood experiences in Illinois. For example, "The Jar" (*Weird Tales*, 1944) is based on the first time that Bradbury saw a pickled embryo, which was displayed in a sideshow at one of the carnivals visiting his hometown. "Homecoming" (*Mademoiselle*, 1946) was inspired by his relatives' marvelous Halloween parties, and "Uncle Einar" (*Dark Carnival*, 1947), a story about a man with green wings, is based loosely on one of Bradbury's uncles.

In 1947, after *Dark Carnival* (a collection of weird and macabre stories) was published, Bradbury turned to another kind of writing — philosophical science fiction. One work in particular, *The Martian Chronicles* (1950), grew out of Bradbury's own personal philosophy and his concern for the future of humankind. *The Martian Chronicles* reflects some of the prevailing anxieties of America in the early atomic age of the 1950's: the fear of nuclear war, the longing for a simpler life, reactions against racism and censorship, and the fear of foreign political powers.

Two other highly personal works, *Dandelion Wine* (1957) and *Something Wicked This Way Comes* (1962), also exemplify his belief that writing should come from a writer's own philosophy and from his or her own experiences. These novels are set in fictitious Green Town — which is, in reality, Bradbury's hometown of Waukegan, Illinois. The ravine described in both books is located on Yeoman Creek, and the library, which is an important setting in *Something Wicked This Way Comes*, was once located on Waukegan's Sheridan Road.

In his later years, Bradbury lived in Los Angeles, was a Sunday painter, and collected Mexican artifacts. He continued writing and lecturing most often on college campuses. He had four grown daughters and several grandchildren. Among Bradbury's later works are *Death Is a Lonely Business* (1985), *The April Witch* (1987), *Death Has Lost Its Charm* (1987), *The Toynbee Convector* (1988), *Graveyard for*

Lunatics (1990), *Folon's Folons* (1990), *Zen in the Art of Writing: Essays on Creativity* (1991), *A Chrestomathy of Ray Bradbury: A Dramatic Selection* (1991), *Yestermorrow: Obvious Answers to Impossible Futures* (1991), *Green Shadows, White Whale* (1992), *The Stars* (1993), *Quicker Than The Eye* (1996), *Driving Blind* (1997), *Dogs Think That Every Day Is Christmas* (1997), and *With Cat for Comforter* (1997). Ray Bradbury died on June 5, 2012. He was 91.

Honors and Achievements

In addition to Bradbury's many books and his hundreds of short stories, works such as *The Beast from 20,000 Fathoms*, *Fahrenheit 451*, *The Illustrated Man*, and *Something Wicked This Way Comes* have been made into major motion pictures. In addition, Bradbury has written for television, radio, and the theater.

Ray Bradbury's work was included in the Best American Short Story collections (1946, 1948, and 1952). He was awarded the O. Henry Memorial Award, the Benjamin Franklin Award in 1954, the Aviation-Space Writer's Association Award for best space article in an American Magazine in 1967, the World Fantasy Award for lifetime achievement, and the Grand Master Award from the Science Fiction Writers of America. His animated film about the history of flight, *Icarus Montgolfier Wright*, was nominated for an academy award, and his teleplay of *The Halloween Tree* won an Emmy. Since 1985, he adapted forty-two of his short stories for *The Ray Bradbury Television Theater* on USA Cable.

Ray Bradbury's writing has been honored in many ways, but perhaps the most unusual way was when an Apollo astronaut named the Dandelion Crater on the Moon after Bradbury's novel, *Dandelion Wine*.

Outside of his literary achievements, Ray Bradbury was the idea consultant and wrote the basic scenario for the United States Pavilion at the 1964 New York World's Fair. He conceived the metaphors for Spaceship Earth, EPCOT, Disney World, and he contributed to the conception of the Orbitron space ride at Euro-Disney, France. He was a creative consultant for the Jon Jerde Partnership, the architectural firm that blueprinted the Glendale Galleria, The Westside Pavilion in Los Angeles, and Horton Plaza in San Diego.

In a field that thrives on the fantastic and the marvelous, Ray Bradbury's best stories celebrate the everyday; in a field preoccupied with the future, Bradbury's vision is firmly rooted in the past. This particular style is evident from the influence of his childhood on his writing (*Dandelion Wine* and *Something Wicked This Way Comes*), as well as from growing up in Illinois. Widely regarded as the most important figure in the development of science fiction as a literary genre, Ray Bradbury's work evokes the themes of racism, censorship, technology, nuclear war, humanistic values, and the importance of imagination.

Clearly, Bradbury kept his promise to Mr. Electrico. He did become a magician, using his pen as a magic wand to transport his readers into wondrous situations. Bradbury himself attests to this fact in an article appearing in the 1952 *Ray Bradbury Review*. He says that he simply transferred his "methods of magic from the stage to a sheet of Eaton's Bond paper — for there is something of the magician in every writer, flourishing his effects and making his miracles."

SUMMARY AND ANALYSIS

Part 1

Summary

In the first part of *Fahrenheit 451*, the character Guy Montag, a thirty-year-old fireman in the twenty-fourth century (remember that the novel was written in the early 1950s) is introduced. In this *dystopian* (dreadful and oppressive) setting, people race "jet cars" down the roads as a way of terminating stress, "parlor walls" are large screens in every home used dually for entertainment and governmental propaganda, and houses have been fireproofed, thus making the job of firemen, as they are commonly known, obsolete. However, firemen have been given a new occupation; they are burners of books and the official censors of the state. As a fireman, Guy Montag is responsible for destroying not only the books he finds, but also the homes in which he finds them. Books are not to be read; they are to be destroyed without question.

For Montag, "It was a pleasure to burn." The state mandated that all books must burn. Therefore, Montag, along with the other firemen, burn the books to show conformity. Without ideas, everyone conforms, and as a result, everyone should be happy. When books and new ideas are available to people, conflict and unhappiness occur. At first, Montag believes that he is happy. When he views himself in the firehouse mirror after a night of burning, he grins "the fierce grin of all men singed and driven back by flame."

However, the reader quickly notices that everything isn't as Montag wants it to be. When Montag meets Clarisse McClellan, his new vivacious teenage neighbor, he begins to question whether he really is happy. Clarisse gives Montag enlightenment; she questions him not only about his own personal happiness but also about his occupation and about the fact that he knows little truth about history. At the same time, she also gives the reader the opportunity to see that the government has dramatically changed what its citizens perceive as their history. For example, Montag never knew that firemen used to fight actual fires or that billboards used to be only 20 feet long. Nor did Montag know that people could actually talk to one another; the governmental use of parlor walls has eliminated the need for casual conversation. Clarisse arouses Montag's curiosity and begins to help him discover that real happiness has been missing from his life for quite some time.

After Montag's encounter with Clarisse, he returns home to find his wife Mildred Montag (Millie) unconscious; she is lying on the bed with her Seashell Radios in her ears and has overdosed on tranquilizers and sleeping pills. Two impersonal technicians, who bring machines to pump her stomach and provide a total transfusion, save Millie, but she could possibly overdose again and never even know it — or so it may seem. The matter of the overdose — whether an attempted suicide or a result of sheer mindlessness — is never settled. Although Montag wishes to discuss the matter of the overdose, Millie does not, and their inability to agree on even this matter suggests the profound estrangement that exists between them.

Even though Montag and Millie have been married for years, Montag realizes, after the overdose incident, that he doesn't really know much about his wife at all. He can't remember when or where he first met her. In fact, all that he does know about his wife is that she is interested only in her "family" — the illusory images on her three-wall TV — and the fact that she drives their car with high-speed abandon. He realizes that their life together is meaningless and purposeless. They don't love each other; in fact, they probably don't love anything, except perhaps burning (Montag) and living secondhand through an imaginary family (Millie).

When Montag returns to work the next day, he touches the Mechanical Hound and hears a growl. The Mechanical Hound is best described as a device of terror, a machine that is perversely similar to a trained killer dog but has been improved by refined technology, which allows it to inexorably track down and capture criminals by stunning them with a tranquilizer. Montag fears that the dog can sense his growing unhappiness. He also fears that the Hound somehow knows that he's confiscated some books during one of his raids.

The fire chief, Captain Beatty also senses Montag's unhappiness. Upon entering the upper level of the firehouse, Montag questions whether the Mechanical Hound can think. Beatty, who functions as the apologist of the dystopia, points out that the Hound "doesn't think anything we don't want it to think." Instantly, Beatty is suspicious of this sudden curiosity in Montag and questions whether Montag feels guilty about something.

After several more days of encountering Clarisse and working at the firehouse, Montag experiences two things that make him realize that he must convert his life. The first incident is one in which he is called to an unidentified woman's house to destroy her books. Her neighbor discovered her cache of books, so they must be burned. The woman stubbornly refuses to leave her home; instead, she chooses to burn with her books. The second incident, which occurs later the same evening, is when Millie tells Montag that the McClellans have moved away because Clarisse died in an automobile accident — she was "run over by a car."

If the Hound and Captain Beatty are a gauge of Montag's growing "disease" (Bradbury's word), the news of Clarisse's death, coupled with a fire call to the unidentified woman's house, brings about his conversion. Montag decides to talk with Millie about his dissatisfaction with his job as a fireman and about the intrinsic values that a person can obtain from books. Suddenly, he sees that Millie is incapable of understanding what he means. All she knows is that books are unlawful and that anyone who breaks the law must be punished. Fearing for her own safety, Millie declares that she is innocent of any wrongdoing, and she says that Montag must leave her alone.

After this confrontation with Millie, Montag entertains the idea of quitting his job, but instead, he decides to feign illness and goes to bed. When Captain Beatty, who is already suspicious of Montag's recent behavior, finds that Montag hasn't come to work, he makes a sick call to Montag's home. Beatty gives Montag a pep talk, explaining to him that every fireman sooner or later goes through a period of intellectual curiosity and steals a book. (Beatty seems to know, miraculously, that Montag stole a book — or books.) Beatty emphatically stresses that books contain nothing believable. He attempts to convince Montag that they are merely stories — fictitious lies — about nonexistent people. He tells Montag that because each person is angered by at least some kind of literature, the simplest solution is to get rid of all books. Ridding the world of controversy puts an end to dispute and allows people to "stay happy all the time." Beatty even supports a sort of perverse democratic ideal: Ridding the world of all controversial books and ideas makes all men equal — each man is the image of other men. He concludes his lecture by assuring Montag that the book-burning profession is an honorable one and instructs Montag to return to work that evening.

Immediately following Beatty's visit, Montag confesses to Mildred that, although he can't explain why, he has stolen, not just one book, but a small library of books for himself during the past year (the total is nearly 20 books, one of which is a Bible). He then begins to reveal his library, which he's hidden in the air-conditioning system. When Millie sees Montag's cache of books, she panics. Montag tries to convince her that their lives are already in such a state of disrepair that an investigation of books may be beneficial. Millie is unconvinced. What neither of them know is that the Mechanical Hound (probably sent by Captain Beatty) is already on Montag's trail, seemingly knowing Montag's mind better than Montag himself.

Analysis

Fahrenheit 451 is currently Bradbury's most famous written work of social criticism. It deals with serious problems of control of the masses by the media, the banning of books, and the suppression of the mind (with censorship). The novel examines a few pivotal days of a man's life, a man who is a burner of books and, therefore, an instrument of suppression. This man (Montag) lives in a world where the past has been destroyed by kerosene-spewing hoses and government brainwashing methods. In a few short days, this man is transformed from a narrow-minded and prejudiced conformist into a dynamic individual committed to social change and to a life of saving books rather than destroying them.

Before you begin the novel, note the significance of the title, 451 degrees Fahrenheit, "the temperature at which book paper catches fire, and burns." Also note the epigram by Juan Ramon Jimenez: "If they give you ruled paper, write the other way." Jimenez (1881-1958) was a Spanish poet who won the Nobel Prize for Literature in 1956 and was largely responsible for introducing Modernism into Spanish poetry. The implications of both concepts — one, a simple fact, and the other, a challenge to authority — gain immense significance by the conclusion of the book.

In the first part of *Fahrenheit 451*, Bradbury uses machine imagery to construct the setting and environment of the book. He introduces Guy Montag, a pyromaniac who took "special pleasure to see things eaten, to see things blackened and changed." He burns books that he hasn't read or even questioned in order to ensure conformity and happiness. Montag has a smile permanently etched on his face; he does not think of the present, the past, or the future. According to his government's views, the only emotion Montag should feel, besides destructive fury, is happiness. He views himself in the mirror after a night of burning and finds himself grinning, and he thinks that all firemen must look like white men masquerading as minstrels, grinning behind their "burnt-corked" masks.

Later, as Montag goes to sleep, he realizes that his smile still grips his face muscles, even in the dark. The language — "fiery smile still gripped by his face muscles" — suggests that his smile is artificial and forced. Soon he will understand that this small bit of truth is an immense truth for himself. At present, Montag seems to enjoy his job as a fireman. He is a "smiling fireman." However, this smile and the later realization of its artificiality foreshadow Montag's eventual dissatisfaction not only with his job but also with his life. Montag smiles, but he is not happy. The smile, just like his "burnt-corked" face, is a mask.

You discover almost immediately (when Montag meets Clarisse McClellan) that he is not happy. By comparing and contrasting the two characters, you can see that Bradbury portrays Clarisse as spontaneous and naturally curious; Montag is insincere and jaded. Clarisse has no rigid daily schedule: Montag is a creature of habit. She speaks to him of the beauties of life, the man in the moon, the early morning dew, and the enjoyment she receives from smelling and looking at things. Montag, however, has never concerned himself with such "insignificant" matters.

Clarisse lives with her mother, father, and uncle; Montag has no family other than his wife, and as you soon discover, his home life is unhappy. Clarisse accepts Montag for what he is; Montag finds Clarisse's peculiarities (that is, her individuality) slightly annoying. "You think too many things," he tells her.

Despite all these differences, the two are attracted to one another. Clarisse's vivacity is infectious, and Montag finds her unusual perspectives about life intriguing. Indeed, she is partly responsible for Montag's change in attitude. She makes Montag think of things that he has never thought of before, and she forces him to consider ideas that he has never contemplated. Moreover, Montag seems to find something in Clarisse that is a long-repressed part of himself: "How like a mirror, too, her face. Impossible; for how many people did you know who refracted your own light to you?"

At the very least, Clarisse awakens in Montag a love and desire to enjoy the simple and innocent things in life. She speaks to him about her delight in letting the rain fall upon her face and into her mouth. Later, Montag, too, turns his head upward into the early November rain in order to catch a mouthful of the cool liquid.

In effect, Clarisse, in a very few meetings, exerts a powerful influence on Montag, and he is never able to find happiness in his former life again.

Yet, if the water imagery of this early scene implies rebirth or regeneration, this imagery is also associated with the artificiality of the peoples' lives in the futuristic dystopia of *Fahrenheit 451*. Each night before she goes to bed, Mildred places small, Seashell Radios into her ears, and the music whisks her away from the dreariness of her everyday reality. As Montag lies in bed, the room seems empty because the waves of sound "came in and bore her [Mildred] off on their great tides of sound, floating her, wide-eyed, toward morning." However, the music that Mildred feels is life-giving actually robs her of the knowledge and meaning of life. She has abandoned reality through her use of these tiny technological wonders that instill mindlessness. The Seashell Radios serve as an escape for Millie because they help her avoid thoughts.

Although she would never — or could never — admit it, Millie Montag isn't happy either. Her need for the Seashell Radios in order to sleep is insignificant when measured against her addiction to tranquilizers and sleeping pills. When Millie overdoses on sleeping pills (which Bradbury never fully explains as accidental or suicidal), she is saved by a machine and two machinelike men who don't care whether she lives or dies. This machine, which pumps out a person's stomach and replaces blood with a fresh supply, is used to foil up to ten unexplainable suicide attempts a night — a machine that is very telling of the social climate.

Montag comes to realize that their inability to discuss the suicide attempt suggests the profound estrangement that exists between them. He discovers that their marriage is in shambles. Neither he nor Millie can remember anything about their past together, and Millie is more interested in her three-wall television family. The TV is another means that Mildred uses to escape reality (and, perhaps, her unhappiness with life and with Montag). She neglects Montag and lavishes her attention instead upon her television relatives. The television family that never says or does anything significant, the high-speed abandon with which she drives their car, and even the overdose of sleeping pills are all indicators for Montag that their life together is meaningless.

For Montag, these discoveries are difficult to express; he is only dimly cognizant of his unhappiness — and Millie's — when he has the first incident with the Mechanical Hound. In some sense, the Hound's distrust of Montag — its growl — is a barometer of Montag's growing unhappiness.

Captain Beatty intuitively senses Montag's growing discontent with his life and job. Beatty is an intelligent but ultimately cynical man. He is, paradoxically, well-read and is even willing to allow Montag to have some slight curiosity about what the books contain. However, Beatty, as a defender of the state (one who has compromised his morality for social stability), believes that all intellectual curiosity and hunger for knowledge must be quelled for the good of the state — for conformity. He even allows for the perversion of history as it appears in *Firemen of America*: "Established, 1790, to burn English-influenced books in the Colonies. First Fireman: Benjamin Franklin. . . " Beatty can tolerate curiosity about books as long as it doesn't affect one's actions. When the curiosity for books begins to affect an individual's conduct and a person's ability to conform — as it does Montag's — the curiosity must be severely punished.

When Montag is called to an unidentified woman's house "in the ancient part of the city," he is amazed to find that the woman will not abandon her home or her books. The woman is clearly a martyr, and her martyrdom profoundly affects Montag. Before she is burned, the woman makes a strange yet significant statement: "Play the man, Master Ridley; we shall this day light such a candle, by God's grace, in England, as I trust shall never be put out." Nicholas Ridley, the Bishop of London in the sixteenth century, was an early martyr for the Protestant faith. He was convicted of heresy and sentenced to burn at the stake with a fellow heretic, Hugh Latimer. Latimer's words to Ridley are the ones that the unidentified woman alludes to before she is set aflame. (Note that a couple visual metaphors for knowledge were traditionally of a woman, sometimes bathed in bright light or holding a burning torch.) Ironically, the woman's words are prophetic; through her own death by fire, Montag's discontent drives him to an investigation of what books really are, what they contain, and what fulfillment they offer.

Montag is unable to understand the change that is taking place within him. With a sickening awareness, he realizes that "[a]lways at night the alarm comes. Never by day! Is it because fire is prettier by night? More spectacle, a better show?" He questions why this particular fire call was such a difficult one to make, and he wonders why his hands seem like separate entities, hiding one of the woman's books under his coat. Her stubborn dignity compels him to discover for himself what is in books.

If Clarisse renews his interest in the sheer excitement of life and Mildred reveals to him the unhappiness of an individual's existence in his society, the martyred woman represents for Montag the power of ideas and, hence, the power of books that his society struggles to suppress.

When Mildred tells Montag that the McClellans moved away because Clarisse died in an automobile accident, Montag's dissatisfaction with his wife, his marriage, his job, and his life intensifies. As he becomes more aware of his unhappiness, he feels even more forced to smile the fraudulent, tight-mouthed smile that he has been wearing. He also realizes that his smile is beginning to fade.

When Montag first entertains the idea of quitting his job for awhile because Millie offers him no sympathetic understanding, he feigns illness and goes to bed. (In all fairness, however, Montag feels sick because he burned the woman alive the night before. His sickness is, so to speak, his conscience weighing upon him.)

Captain Beatty, as noted earlier, has been suspicious of Montag's recent behavior, but he isn't aware of the intellectual and moral changes going on in Montag. However, he recognizes Montag's discontent, so he visits Montag. He tells Montag that books are figments of the imagination. Fire is good because it eliminates the conflicts that books can bring. Montag later concludes that Beatty is actually afraid of books and masks his fear with contempt. In effect, his visit is a warning to Montag not to allow the books to seduce him.

Notice that Beatty repeatedly displays great knowledge of books and reading throughout this section. Obviously, he is using his knowledge to combat and twist the doubts that Montag is experiencing. In fact, Beatty points out that books are meaningless, because man as a creature is satisfied as long as he is entertained and not left uncertain about anything. Books create too much confusion because the intellectual pattern for man is "out of the nursery into the college and back to the nursery." Therefore, books disrupt the regular intellectual pattern of man because they lack definitive clarity.

Another interesting point discussed by Beatty in this section is how people view death. While discussing death, Beatty points out, "Ten minutes after death a man's a speck of black dust. Let's not quibble over individuals with memoriums." Beatty, therefore, introduces the idea that death isn't something that people mourn at this time. Also in this discussion between Beatty and Montag, the reader can question whether Clarisse's death was accidental, as Beatty states, "queer ones like her don't happen often. We know how to nip most of them in the bud, early."

The major developments of Part One surround the degenerated future in which books and independent thinking are forbidden. Notice, however, Bradbury's implicit hope and faith in the common man by representing the life of a working-class fireman. Though Montag isn't a man of profound thought or speech, his transformation has occurred through his innate sense of morality and growing awareness of human dignity.

Note, as well, the dual image of fire in its destructive and purifying functions. Although fire is destructive, it also warms; hence, the source of the title of Part One, "The Hearth and the Salamander." Hearth suggests home and the comforting aspect of fire — its ability to warm and cook. In ancient mythology, the salamander was a creature that could survive fire. Possibly Montag himself is represented in the salamander reference. His job dictates that he live in an environment of fire and destruction, but Montag realizes that the salamander is able to remove itself from fire — and survive.

Glossary

this great python the fire hose, which resembles a great serpent; a key image in the novel that serves as a reminder of Adam and Eve's temptation to disobey God in the Garden of Eden.

451 degrees Fahrenheit the temperature at which book paper catches fire and burns.

pigeon-winged books the books come alive and flap their "wings" as they are thrown into the fire. This connection between books and birds continues throughout the text and symbolizes enlightenment through reading.

black beetle-colored helmet in literature, the beetle, with its prominent black horns, is a symbol for Satan. Here, vehicles resemble beetles in the dystopian society.

infinitely lacking limits or bounds; extending beyond measure or comprehension.

salamander a mythological reptile, resembling a lizard, that was said to live in fire. In the concept of nature, the salamander is a visual representation of fire. In mythology, it endures the flames without burning.

phoenix in Egyptian mythology, a lone bird that lives in the Arabian desert for 500 or 600 years and then sets itself on fire, rising renewed from the ashes to start another long life; a symbol of immortality.

Clarisse the girl's name derives from the Latin word for *brightest*.

Guy Montag his name suggests two significant possibilities — Guy Fawkes, the instigator of a plot to blow up the English Houses of Parliament in 1605, and Montag, a trademark of Mead, an American paper company, which makes stationery and furnaces.

man in the moon the perception of children that the contours of the moon's surface are a face, which peers down at them. The image reflects the oppressive nature of a society that burns books because the man in the moon is always watching them.

mausoleum a large, imposing tomb; often a symbol of death used in literature. Used to describe the interior of Guy's bedroom.

moonstones an opal, or a milky-white feldspar with a pearly luster, used as a gem. The moonstone is connected with Mercury, the mythological guide who leads souls to the underworld.

black cobra the "suction snake" that pumps Mildred's stomach repeats the earlier image of the python; the impersonal handymen who operate it have "eyes of puff adders." The fact that it has an eye suggests a sinister and invasive fiber optic tube that examines the inside of the body's organs and even the soul.

electronic bees futuristic "seashell ear-thimbles" that block out thoughts and supplant them with mindless entertainment.

TV parlor a multidimensional media family that draws the viewer into action, thereby supplanting the viewer's real family.

That's what the lady said snappy stage comeback that Mildred uses in place of normal conversation.

proboscis a tubular organ for sensing; nose or snout.

morphine or procaine a sedative and an anesthetic.

Beatty the fire captain, who "baits" Montag, is well-named.

November 4 the firemen play cards early on Mischief Day (November 4), the eve of Guy Fawkes Day, when bonfires and burning of guys in effigy commemorate his Gunpowder Plot, an abortive attempt to destroy James I and his Protestant supporters, who oppressed Catholics.

Stoneman and Black firemen whose names suggest that the hardness of their hearts and the color of their skin and hair come from contact with smoke.

Benjamin Franklin founder of America's first fire company in Boston in 1736.

Play the man, Master Ridley; we shall this day light such a candle, by God's grace, in England, as I trust shall never be put out! Bishops Hugh Latimer and Nicholas Ridley, Protestant supporters of the late Queen Jane Grey, were burned at the stake for heresy at Oxford on October 16, 1555. They refused to endorse Queen Mary, a Catholic, claiming that she was an illegitimate daughter of Henry VIII, born after he married his late brother's wife, Catherine of Aragon. Later, Captain Beatty recites the latter portion of the quotation and indicates that he knows something of history.

cricket English slang for fair play; sportsmanship.

Time has fallen asleep in the afternoon sunshine from Chapter 1 of *Dreamthorp*, a collection of essays by Alexander Smith, a Glasgow lacemaker.

Tower of Babel in Genesis 11:1-9, the mythic explanation of how Noah's children came to speak different languages. The word *babel* means a confusion of voices, languages, or sounds.

centrifuge the sight of being spun in a great gyre delineates Montag's impression of separation from reality.

cacophony harsh, jarring sound; mindless noise.

pratfall slang for a fall on the buttocks, especially one for comic effect, as in burlesque.

automatic reflex Beatty uses this term to describe how people stopped using their brains and began depending on nerve functions that require no thought.

theremin named after Russian inventor Leon Theremin; an early electronic musical instrument whose tone and loudness are controlled by moving the hands in the air between two projecting antennas.

our fingers in the dike an allusion to the legend about the Dutch boy who performed a noble, selfless public service in holding back the sea by keeping his finger in a hole in the dike.

It is computed that eleven thousand persons have at several times suffered death rather than submit to break their eggs at the smaller end Jonathan Swift illustrates the pettiness of human controversy in Book I, Chapter 4 of *Gulliver's Travels*. The satire found in Swift's writing emphasizes the absurd extent to which society will go to enforce conformity. When Montag reads this quote to Millie, he is pointing out that people are willing to die rather than conform, even though others may believe their position to be absurd or irrational.

Part 2

Summary

Millie and Montag spend the rest of the cold, rainy, November afternoon reading through the books that Montag has acquired. As Montag reads, he begins to understand what Clarisse meant when she said that she knew the way that life is to be experienced. So entranced are Montag and Millie by the substance of the books, they ignore the noise of a sniffing dog outside their window.

In Millie's mind, books hold no value; she would rather avoid reality and bask in the fantasy of her television. Although she can choose books and life, she chooses instead to place her loyalties with the television character, White Clown, and the rest of her television family. Montag, however, needs to find someone from whom he can learn and discuss what the books are trying to tell him; he needs a teacher.

In his desperation and thirst for knowledge, Montag recalls an encounter last year with an elderly man in the park. The old man, a retired English professor named Faber, made an impression on Montag because he actually spoke with Montag about real things. Montag remembers that he keeps Faber's phone number in his files of possible book hoarders, and he determines that if anyone can be his teacher and help him understand books, Faber can. Consequently, Montag takes the subway to Faber's home and carries with him a copy of the Bible.

Faber is a devotee of the ideas contained in books. He is also concerned with the common good of man. Montag immediately senses Faber's enthusiasm and readily admits his feelings of unhappiness and emptiness. He confesses that his life is missing the values of books and the truths that they teach. Montag then asks Faber to teach him to understand what he reads. At first, Faber views this new teaching assignment as a useless, as well as dangerous, undertaking. His attitude, however, does not deter Faber from launching into such a challenging and exciting task.

Nevertheless, Faber is skeptical and pessimistic of whether books can help their society. As if responding to Faber's pessimism, Montag presents Faber with an insidious plan that entails hiding books in the homes of firemen so even they will become suspect. Ultimately, through supposed treason, the firehouses themselves will burn. Faber acknowledges the cleverness of the plan, but cynically, he urges Montag to return home and give up his newly acquired rebelliousness.

Faber's demonstration of cowardice and political nihilism incites Montag to begin ripping pages out of the Bible. Shocked by the destruction of this rare, precious book and stirred by Montag's rebellious convictions, Faber agrees to help him.

As a result of Montag's concern about how he will act when he and Beatty next meet, Faber shows Montag one of his inventions — a two-way, Seashell Radio-like communication device that resembles a small green bullet and fits into the ear. Through the use of this device, Faber can be in constant contact with Montag, and he promises to support him if Beatty attempts to intimidate Montag. Through the use of Faber's spying invention, they listen to Captain Beatty together.

Throughout Part Two, the threat of war increases. Ten million men have been mobilized, and the people expect victory. Montag's war is just beginning.

After his meeting with Faber, Montag returns home hoping to discuss ideas and books with Millie. Unfortunately, in Montag's case, a little learning is dangerous thing, because when he returns home, he finds company. Immediately, he launches into a tirade in the presence of two of Millie's human friends, Mrs. Phelps and Mrs. Bowles. This tirade will prove costly to his idealistic plans.

Montag, who is tired of listening to the women's meaningless triviality, decides to disconnect the television and begins to attempt a discussion with the women. He reads Matthew Arnold's "Dover Beach" in hopes that the women will be motivated to discuss the work. Although the women — especially Mrs. Phelps — are moved by the poem, they can't say why and dismiss any further discussion.

Faber attempts, through the two-way radio, to calm Montag's zealous anger. He urges Montag to make believe, to say that he is joking, and Faber commands him to throw his book of poems into the incinerator. Despite Faber's admonitions and Millie's defensive maneuvers, Montag continues by soundly cursing Mrs. Phelps and Mrs. Bowles for their empty and corrupt lives. Mrs. Bowles leaves in a fury; Mrs. Phelps, in tears. Characteristically, Millie escapes from this horrible scene by rushing to the bathroom and downing several pills. She wants to sleep and forget. Montag hides several of the remaining books in some bushes in his backyard and then goes off to work. He carries with him a substitute book to give Beatty in place of the Bible that he left with Faber.

Montag dreads the meeting with Beatty, even though Faber promises to be with him via the two-way radio implanted in Montag's ear. Beatty tries to coax Montag into admitting his crime of stealing (and reading) books, but Faber is true to his word and supports Montag during Beatty's taunting.

Before Montag can respond to Beatty's tirade, the fire alarm sounds, and the firemen rush off to work. Ironically, Montag realizes that his own home is the firemen's target.

Analysis

While Millie and Montag are reading, Clarisse's profound influence on Montag becomes obvious. In fact, Montag points out that "She was the first person I can remember who looked straight at me as if I counted." However, Millie and Montag have forgotten — or are ignoring — the danger of their situation. They hear "a faint scratching" outside the front door and "a slow, probing sniff, and exhalation of electric steam" under the doorsill. Millie's reaction is "It's only a dog." Only a dog? The Mechanical Hound lurks outside, probably programmed by Beatty to collect evidence that he can use later against Montag.

The Montags, however, can't ignore the sounds of bombers crossing the sky over their house, signaling the imminence of war. Although no on knows the cause of the war or its origins, the country is filled with unrest, which is a parallel to the growing unrest and anger smoldering within Montag.

Abandonment of reality has become uppermost in Millie's mind. When Montag speaks to her about the value and merit in books, she shrieks and condemns him for possessing the books. Bradbury describes her as "sitting there like a wax doll melting in its own heat." Here, fire imagery again implies destruction. This time, however, Millie carries the seeds of her own destruction. As stated earlier at the end of Part One, she can choose books (and life). But because she shuns books and the lessons that she can learn from them, Bradbury describes her as a doll that melts in its self-generated heat. Montag, on the other hand, wants to comprehend the information that the books give him. More importantly, however, Montag realizes that he needs a teacher if he wants to fully understand the books' information.

The person to whom Montag chooses to turn, Faber, "had been thrown out upon the world forty years ago when the last liberal arts college shut for lack of students and patronage." Montag recalls from their earlier encounter Faber's "cadenced voice" and "convictions"; in particular, Faber's words seemed a great deal like poetry. He said to Montag, "I don't talk *things*, sir; I talk the *meaning* of things. I sit here and *know* I'm alive."

While riding the subway to Faber's house, Montag experiences a moment of self-reflection. He discovers that his smile, "the old burnt-in smile," has disappeared. He recognizes his emptiness and unhappiness. Moreover, he recognizes his lack of formal education — what he thinks is his essential ignorance. This sense of helplessness, of ineffectuality, of powerlessness, of his utter inability to comprehend what is in books, overwhelms him, and his mind flashes back to a time when he was a child on the seashore "trying to fill a sieve with sand." Montag recalls that "the faster he poured [the sand], the faster it sifted through with a hot whispering." He now has this same feeling of helplessness as he reads the Bible; his mind seems to be a sieve through which the words pass without Montag's comprehending or remembering them. He knows that in a few hours he must give this precious book to Beatty, so he attempts to read and memorize the scriptures — in particular, Jesus' Sermon on the Mount. As he attempts to memorize the passages, however, a loud and brassy advertisement for "Denham's Dental Detergent" destroys his concentration.

Montag is trying to rebel, but he is confused because of his many mental blocks against nonconformity. He has never before deviated from the norm, and his attempts to establish an individual identity are continually frustrated. Montag's flight to Faber's home is his only hope. The scene represents a man running for his life, which, in fact, Montag is doing, though he doesn't fully realize it yet. Nor does he know that he is already an outcast. He can never return to his former existence. His transformation is inevitable.

Of significance in this part of the book is that Faber bears a close resemblance to Carl Jung's archetypal figure of the "old man." According to Jung in his essay "The Phenomenology of the Spirit in Fairy Tales," the old man archetype represents, on the one hand, knowledge, reflection, insight, wisdom, cleverness, and intuition, and on the other hand, he represents such moral qualities as good will and readiness to help, which makes his "spiritual" character sufficiently plain. Faber displays these qualities, and he, like Clarisse, is associated with the color white, symbolic of his spiritual nature: "He [Faber] and the white plaster walls inside were much the same. There was white in the flesh of his mouth and his cheeks and his hair was white and his eyes had faded, with white in the vague blueness there." The color white is significant here because it indicates purity and goodness. White is also the opposite of the blackness of the burnt books and the dark ashes into which they are burned.

Besides enlightening Montag, Faber expands on his philosophy about the use of the books, as well as about society in general. (One can't help but think that Faber's discussion is close to Bradbury's own view, but of course, this assertion is simply speculation.) Faber explains that books have "quality" and "texture," that they reveal stark reality, not only the pleasant aspect of life but also the bad aspects of life: "They show the pores in the face of life," and their society finds this discomforting. Tragically, society has started programming thoughts: People are no longer allowed leisure time to think for themselves. Faber insists that leisure is essential to achieving proper appreciation of books. (By "leisure," Faber doesn't mean "off hours," the time away from work, but simply ample time to think about things beyond one's self.) Distractions, such as the all-encompassing television walls, simply will not allow for leisure time. Ultimately, however, Faber thinks that the truth in books can never be of value in this society again unless its individuals have "the right to carry out actions based on" what they find in the books. Books are of value only when people are allowed the freedom to act upon what they've learned. On this last point, Faber is pessimistic; he is convinced that people in his society will never have the freedom to act upon what they've learned.

When Montag presents Faber with his plan to incite revenge upon the other firemen, Faber is skeptical because "firemen are rarely necessary"; their destruction would hardly warrant a change in society. Faber means that "So few want to be rebels anymore." People are too distracted — that is, too "happy" — to want to change things.

After Faber decides to join Montag in his plight, Bradbury later describes this coalition of two as "Montag-plus-Faber, fire plus water." Fire and water images blend, because the product resulting from the union of these two separate and opposite items is a third product — wine. Wine looks like water, but it burns like fire. Montag and Faber work together, because all is far from well in the world.

By joining Montag, Faber also states that he will be, in effect, "the Queen Bee," remaining safely in the hive; Montag is "the drone." Before parting, they initiate plans to "[print] a few books, and wait on the war to break the pattern and give us the push we need. A few bombs and the 'families' in the walls of all the homes, like harlequin rats, will shut up!" Perhaps this subversion (the destruction of TV) will restore the public's interest in books. However, despite his decision to help Montag, Faber acknowledges that he is ultimately a coward. He will stay safe at home while Montag faces the threat of punishment.

As the threat of war increases, you can see that the war is a parallel to Montag's attitude concerning his own personal battle. His inner turmoil intensifies. Armed with a friend such as Faber, the two-way green-bullet radio, and a beginner's knowledge of the true value of books, he is now ready to wage war against Beatty and the rest of his stagnant society. Montag feels that he is becoming a new man, intoxicated by his newfound inner strength, but his is an idealistic knowledge blended with the zealousness of a convert; he has not considered any sort of pragmatic implementation plan.

When Montag meets with Mrs. Phelps and Mrs. Bowles, he forgets that they are a good deal like Millie; they are devoted to their television families, they are politically enervated, and they show little interest in the imminent war. Because their husbands are routinely called away to war, the women are unconcerned. War has happened before and it may happen again.

Listening to their empty babble, animated by his rebel posture, and with Faber whispering comfortably in his ear, Montag impulsively shouts, "Let's talk." He begins reading from "Dover Beach" by Matthew Arnold:

Ah, love, let us be true

To one another! for the world, which seems

To lie before us like a land of dreams,

So various, so beautiful, so new,

Hath really neither joy, nor love, nor light,

Nor certitude, nor peace, nor help for pain;

And we are here as on a darkling plain

Swept with confused alarms of struggle and flight,

Where ignorant armies clash by night.

Despite their flippancy and chatter, the women are moved, but again, they do not understand why. Although Mildred makes the choice of what her husband should read, Matthew Arnold's poem typifies Montag's pessimism as he tries to fathom the vapid, purposeless lifestyles of the three women. The poem forces the women to respond — Mrs. Phelps with tears and Mrs. Bowles with anger. The Cheshire catlike smiles that Millie and her friends wear indicate their illusion of happiness. Montag imagines these smiles as burning through the walls of the house. Ironically, smiles should signify joy, but not in this case, just as they did not in Montag's case. However, the smiles of these women are destructive and perhaps evil. Furthermore, Millie and her friends are characterized by fire imagery; they light cigarettes and blow the smoke from their mouths. They all have "sun-fired" hair and "blazing" fingernails. They, like the fleet of firemen, are headed toward their own destruction.

After this disastrous situation with Millie, Mrs. Phelps, and Mrs. Bowles, Montag anxiously prepares for his meeting with Beatty. Captain Beatty's suspicion of Montag steadily increases as he watches Montag with an "alcohol-flame stare." While Beatty is baiting Montag to slip about stealing books, Faber proves himself to be a good partner to Montag and supports him throughout the entire confrontation. In a most striking diatribe, Beatty reveals that he is extremely well read; he accurately quotes authors from a wide range of historical periods and is able to apply what he has read. He has obviously thought about what the works mean and, in a curious way, uses them to good effect against Montag. He is aware of Montag's newfound zealousness (as Beatty states, "Read a few lines and off you go over a cliff. Bang, you're ready to blow up the world, chop off heads, knock down women and children, destroy authority,") and manages to urge Montag in a direction that would cause him to abandon his recently acquired humanistic convictions. Through ignoring the title of the book returned by Montag, Beatty shows that he is aware of Montag's collection and is trying to get Montag to admit his guilt. Also, Beatty wants to prove to Montag that the title (and the book itself) is not significant. The only important point about the book is that it needs to be destroyed.

Montag can't respond to Beatty's denunciation of him (no doubt his rebuttal would have failed miserably) because the fire alarm sounds. In a colossal act of irony, Montag realizes when the firemen are called to action that his own home is the target for the firemen. Instead of implementing a plan to undermine the firemen by planting books in their houses, Montag, in a grotesque reversal of expectations, becomes a victim himself.

Part Two centers on Montag's first personal experience with ideas found in books, and it details his change into a social rebel. The section seemingly ends on a note of defeat.

Glossary

We cannot tell the precise moment when friendship is formed. As in filling a vessel drop by drop, there is at last a drop which makes it run over; so in a series of kindnesses there is at last one which makes the heart run over from James Boswell's *Life of Dr. Johnson*, published in 1791. The quotation helps Montag understand his relationship with the mysterious Clarisse, who brings joy into his life for no obvious reason.

That favorite subject. Myself. taken from a letter of the British biographer James Boswell, dated July 16, 1763. The quotation emphasizes the chasm that separates Montag from Mildred, who shuns self-analysis and submerges herself in drugs and the television programs that sedate her mind.

half out of the cave Bradbury alludes to Plato's cave allegory, found in Book 7 of his *Republic*. The analogy describes how people rely on flickering shadows as their source of reality.

Faber the character's name suggests that of Peter Faber (1506-1545), tutor of Ignatius Loyola and founder of two Jesuit colleges.

Mr. Jefferson? Mr. Thoreau?Thomas Jefferson, the chief author of the Declaration of Independence, and Henry David Thoreau, author of *Walden* and *Civil Disobedience*. This phrase is used to illustrate that all books and authors are valuable. These two authors are chosen to show who wrote about revolution and fighting opression.

dentrifice any preparation for cleaning teeth. This word is part of the phrase that Montag hears repeatedly in the subway.

Consider the lilies of the field. They toil not, neither do they In his surreal dash on the subway toward Faber's house, Montag tries to read a line from Jesus' Sermon on the Mount from the Gospel of St. Matthew. The line, which is taken from Chapter 6, verses 28-29, concludes, "And yet I say unto you, that even Solomon in all his glory was not arrayed like one of these." This quotation reminds Montag that spiritual hunger is greater than material need.

Caesar's praetorian guard a reference to the bodyguards that surrounded the Roman Caesars, beginning with Rome's first emperor, Octavian, later named Augustus. While holding back the mob, the praetorians wielded supreme control over the rulers who they sought to protect, and they are thought to have assassinated Caligula and replaced him with Claudius, a crippled historian who was their choice of successor.

the salamander devours its tail Faber, who creates a way to implicate firemen in their own menace and therefore eradicate them, characterizes his plot with an image of self-destruction.

this electronic cowardice Faber, an old man who is too fearful to confront Captain Beatty, is willing to direct Montag's confrontation through his electronic listening and speaking device.

The Book of Job Faber selects this book of the Old Testament, which describes how Job is tested by God. The upshot of Job's struggle with suffering, loss, and temptation is that he learns to trust.

Vesuvius a volcano near Naples that erupted August 24, 79 A.D., burying the citizens of Pompeii and Herculaneum.

Cheshire cat a grinning cat, a character from Chapter 6 of Lewis Carroll's *Alice in Wonderland.*

In again out again Finnegan a common nonsense rhyme indicating Mrs. Phelps' lack of concern about the war and her husband's part in it. The quotation restates "Off again, on again, gone again, Finnegan," a terse telegram about a rail crash from Finnegan (a railroad boss) to Flanagan (his employer).

fire plus water Montag, who perceives the split halves of his being, anticipates the distillation of his fiery self into wine after Faber has molded his intellect with wisdom and teaching.

Who are a little wise, the best fools be a line from John Donne's poem "The Triple Fool," which Beatty uses to confuse and stifle Montag.

the sheep returns to the fold. We're all sheep who have strayed at times Beatty alludes to the prophecy in Isaiah 53:6: "All we like sheep have gone astray; we have turned ever one to his own way; and the Lord hath laid on him the iniquity of us all." The message implies that Montag has betrayed his fellow firemen.

Truth is truth, to the end of reckoning Beatty's montage of quotations rambles on to a verse from Shakespeare's *Measure for Measure,* Act V, Scene i, Line 45.

They are never alone that are accompanied with noble thoughts a verse taken from Sir Philip Sidney's *Arcadia*, which in turn paraphrases a line from Beaumont and Fletcher's *Love's Cure*, Act III, Scene iii.

Sweet food of sweetly uttered knowledge a line from Sir Philip Sidney's *Defense of Poesy*.

Words are like leaves and where they most abound, Much fruit of sense beneath is rarely found Beatty quotes a couplet from Alexander Pope's *Essay on Criticism* as cynical commentary on his profusely garbled and contradictory recitation.

A little learning is a dangerous thing. Drink deep, or taste not the Pierian spring; There shallow draughts intoxicate the brain, and drinking largely sobers us again a famous pair of couplets from Alexander Pope's *Essay on Criticism*, which warns the learner that scholarship requires dedication for maximum effect.

Knowledge is more than equivalent to force an aphorism from Chapter 13 of Dr. Samuel Johnson's *Rasselas*.

He is no wise man that will quit a certainty for an uncertainty an aphorism from Dr. Samuel Johnson's *Idler*.

Truth will come to light, murder will not be hid long! from Shakespeare's *Merchant of Venice*, Act II, Scene ii, Line 86.

Oh God, he speaks only of his horse a paraphrase of "he doth nothing but talk of his horse" from Shakespeare's *Merchant of Venice*, Act I, Scene ii, Lines 37-38.

The Devil can cite Scripture for his purpose from Shakespeare's *Merchant of Venice*, Act I, Scene iii, Line 99.

This age thinks better of a gilded fool, than of a threadbare saint in wisdom's school a couplet from Thomas Dekker's *Old Fortunatus*.

The dignity of truth is lost with much protesting a line from Ben Jonson's *Catiline's Conspiracy*, Act III, Scene ii.

Carcasses bleed at the sight of the murderer a line from Robert Burton's *Anatomy of Melancholy*, Part I, Section I, Member 2, Subsection 5.

trench mouth an infectious disease characterized by ulceration of the mucous membranes of the mouth and throat and caused by a bacterium; derived from its prevalence among soldiers in trenches.

Knowledge is power a line from Francis Bacon's *Advancement of Learning*, Book I, i, 3.

A dwarf on a giant's shoulders sees the furthest of the two from *Democritus to the Reader*, Robert Burton's paraphrase from Lucan's *Civil War*, which is echoed in Sir Isaac Newton's letter to Robert Hooke, February 5, 1675 or 1676.

The folly of mistaking a metaphor for a proof, a torrent of verbiage for a spring of capital truths, and oneself as an oracle is inborn in us a paraphrase of Paul Valery's *Introduction to the Method of Leonardo da Vinci.*

A kind of excellent dumb discourse a line from Shakespeare's *Tempest*, Act III, Scene iii, Line 38.

All's well that is well in the end a paraphrase of Shakespeare's *All's Well That Ends Well*, Act IV, Scene iv, Line 35.

the tyranny of the majority from John Emerich Edward Dalberg-Acton's *History of Freedom and Other Essays.*

Part 3

Summary

In this final section of the book, Montag discovers that Millie turned in the fire alarm (though her friends, Mrs. Phelps and Mrs. Bowles, earlier lodged a complaint that Beatty ignored). While Beatty seems to regret what he must do to Montag, he taunts Montag in a mean-spirited way and reminds Montag that he has given him many warnings about what could happen.

Finally, in his conversation with Montag, Beatty forces Montag to set fire to his own home. Little does he realize that Montag finds a certain perverse satisfaction in torching the interior of his home — especially the television screens.

Meanwhile, Faber continually urges Montag to escape, but Montag is hesitant because the Mechanical Hound is on the prowl. Montag has also fallen into his former way of thinking as a result of Beatty's verbal assaults and the trauma of what has happened to both himself and his home. While Montag hesitates, Beatty discovers the green bullet in his ear and threatens to track the two-way radio to its source (Faber).

As if motivating Montag to take action against him, Beatty taunts Montag relentlessly. In one quick motion, Montag turns the liquid fire on Captain Beatty, who collapses to the pavement.

After pummeling Stoneman and Black, Montag tries to escape, but the Mechanical Hound stuns him in the leg with its procaine needle. In the span of only a few minutes, Montag becomes a criminal, an enemy of the people. He is now a hunted man, sought by the police and the firemen's salamanders. The police, Montag is sure, with the aid of helicopters, will immediately begin a manhunt. The only friend he can turn to is Faber. Only Faber holds some promise for Montag's survival.

Despite the urgency, Montag rescues some of the books that he hid in his backyard (Millie burned most of them, but she missed a few). On his way to Faber's house, Montag discovers that war has been declared upon his town.

In his journey to Faber's, Montag confronts an unforeseen danger: crossing a boulevard. Because the automobiles travel at such high speeds, crossing the street is extremely dangerous — coupled by the fact that, because such little value is given to a person's life, running over pedestrians is a sport. (Recall that Clarisse was killed by a hit-and-run driver.) In Montag's case, the danger is compounded because he has a crippled leg, deadened with procaine.

Despite the danger, Montag has little choice; he must cross the boulevard in order to reach Faber. He must either risk crossing the boulevard or face certain execution in a matter of minutes. As he's crossing the street, one vehicle focuses on Montag's running figure. A fortuitous stumble allows Montag to escape certain death. Unharmed (except for one-sixteenth of an inch of black tire tread on his middle finger), he travels onward.

Montag makes one stop prior to his arrival at Faber's home. He stops at the home of a fellow fireman — Black's house — and hides the books that he has been carrying in Black's kitchen. Because Black was responsible for burning many other people's homes, Montag reasons that Black should have his own home burned. Thus, Montag activates the plan to frame firemen that he had previously sketched for Faber. He phones in a fire alarm and then waits until the blare of the siren is heard before he continues on to Faber's. Black's house will be burned.

Together, Montag and Faber make their plans for escape. Faber tells Montag to try the river. If he can cross it, he should make his way down the railroad tracks leading out of the city. Once out of the city, he will meet up with one of the many groups of exiles forced to flee to the countryside and find refuge with them. As for himself, Faber plans to catch the early morning bus to St. Louis to get in touch with an old printer friend.

While the two men make their plans, the television announces that a massive manhunt has been organized to track down Montag. Faber and Montag discover that a new Mechanical Hound has been introduced to the search and that the networks intend to participate by televising the chase.

With the news that a second Mechanical Hound was brought to the area, Faber and Montag must take careful, precautionary steps to avoid capture. Montag instructs Faber to burn in the incinerator everything that he (Montag) has touched and then rub everything else down with alcohol. He also suggests that Faber cover the scent with moth spray and then hose off the sidewalk and turn on the lawn sprinklers. In this way, they can confuse the Mechanical Hound's sense of smell and cause him to lose Montag's trail into Faber's house; Faber will remain safe while Montag lures the Hound to the river. Before he leaves, he takes a cardboard suitcase filled with some old clothes of Faber's as well as a bottle of whiskey. Montag makes a run for the river, knowing that the Mechanical Hound is still on his trail as helicopters gather and hover overhead.

Montag finally hobbles to the safety of the river undetected, where he douses himself in whiskey and dresses in Faber's clothes. After discarding the suitcase, he plunges into the river and is swept away. While he travels downstream, the Mechanical Hound loses his scent at the river's edge. Undaunted, however, the police refuse to be denied the capture.

The police can't allow the public to know of their failure to snare Montag, so they enact a hoax: An innocent man is chosen as a victim for the TV cameras. The populace is deceived into thinking that Montag is dead because their wall televisions depict the murder of the suspect Montag. (Note that the population has never seen the real Montag.)

While the chase continues elsewhere, Montag floats in the river toward the far shore and safety. In just a few short days, Montag has become a rebel and an outlaw.

As if seeing the world and nature for the first time, Montag continues his journey on land. Half an hour later, he sees a fire in the black distance where he stumbles upon a group of outcasts.

The leader of these outcasts is Granger, a former author and intellectual. Curiously, Granger seems to have expected Montag and reveals his good will by offering him a vial filled with something that alters Montag's perspiration; after Montag drinks the fluid, the Mechanical Hound can no longer track him.

Granger explains to Montag the nature of the commune and how each member chooses a book and memorizes it. After the entire book has been memorized, he burns it to prevent the individual from being arrested by the authorities. From that time on, the story is transmitted verbally from one generation to another.

Montag confesses to Granger that he once memorized some of the Book of Ecclesiastes. Granger tells him that a man named Harris knows the verses from memory, but if anything ever happens to Harris, Montag will become the book.

When Montag admits the grand failure of his plan to plant books in firemen's houses, Granger replies that the plan may have worked had it been carried out on a national scale. Granger feels, however, that the commune's way of giving life to books through their embodiment in people is the best way to combat the censorship of the government.

Because of war (that could begin at any minute), the commune is forced to move south, farther down the river, away from the city that is a sure target of attack. Jets shriek overhead continually, heading for battle. Although Montag thinks briefly of Millie and of his former life, he is forced back to reality when, in an abrupt finale, the city is destroyed.

Shaken by the destruction of the city, Granger, Montag, and the rest of the commune are compelled to return to the city and lend what help they can.

Analysis

The ironies in this book continue to multiply as Montag discovers that Millie was the one who turned in the fire alarm. In fact, it's interesting to note that as Millie makes her abrupt departure, her worries and concern focus only on her television family and not her husband (Montag). Although Beatty feels some remorse over what will happen to Montag, he continues to ridicule him: "Old Montag wanted to fly near the sun and now that he's burnt his damn wings, he wonders why. Didn't I hint enough when I sent the Hound around your place?" Though one's sympathies are, rightly so, with Montag, Beatty is revealed here as a man torn between duty and conscience, which makes him more of an individual and less a villain, less a straw man. He does not particularly want to arrest Montag for breaking the law and his metaphorical concept of Montag as Icarus further reveals his active imagination and knowledge of (illegal) books.

Yet through sheer maliciousness, Beatty demands that Montag burn his own home. However, note that Montag does not burn the television with remorse — in fact, he takes great pleasure in burning it: "And then he came to the parlor where the great idiot monsters lay asleep with their white thoughts and their snowy dreams. And he shot a bolt at each of the three blank walls and the vacuum hissed out at him." In a strange way, Montag gets his revenge on the television screens that he hates so strongly.

The entire episode has, for Montag, a phantasmagorical quality. He perceives his arrival and the preparations for the burning as a "carnival" being set up. Later, after the destruction of his house and after the spectators disappear, Montag remarks that the incident was as if "the great tents of the circus had slumped into charcoal and rubble and the show was well over." After the burning of his house, Montag is not smiling.

With Faber screaming in his ear to escape, Montag experiences a moment of doubt when Beatty reduces Montag's book knowledge to pretentiousness: "Why don't you belch Shakespeare at me, you fumbling snob? . . . Go ahead now, you secondhand literateur, pull the trigger." With the flamethrower in his hand and, in his mind, the seeming futility of ever correcting the ills of society, Montag decides that fire, after all, is probably the best solution for everything. "We never burned *right*," he says.

The meaning of Montag's utterance is open to speculation. At first glance, this statement is about passion: If the firemen have to burn books, they should know the subjects of the books and what information they contain. Or possibly, burning shouldn't be done simply as a mindless job that one does out of habit, but should be done out of political and ideological convictions. Given the context, however, Montag says his line with the implication that Beatty was wrong to encourage burning when he, Beatty, knew the value of books.

As he turns the flamethrower on Beatty, who collapses to the pavement like a "charred wax doll," you can note the superb poetic justice in this action. Beatty always preached to Montag that fire was the solution to everyone's problems ("Don't face a problem, burn it," Beatty told him) and Beatty, himself, is burned as a solution to Montag's problem. Note once again, that in describing Beatty's death, Bradbury uses the image of a wax doll. The imagery of the wax doll is thus used in *Fahrenheit 451* to describe both Beatty and Millie. By using this comparison, Bradbury shows that Beatty and Millie do not appear to be living things; they fit the mold made by a dystopian society. As a result, Beatty is charred and destroyed by the fire that gave purpose and direction to his own life.

Although Montag, who is now a fugitive, feels justified in his actions, he curses himself for taking these violent actions to such an extreme. His discontent shows that he is not a vicious killer, but a man with a conscience.

While Montag stumbles down the alley, a sudden and awesome recognition stops him cold in his tracks: "In the middle of the crying Montag knew it for the truth. Beatty had wanted to die. He had just stood there, not really trying to save himself, just stood there, joking, needling, thought Montag, and the thought was enough to stifle his sobbing and let him pause for air." Instantly, the reader and Montag understand Beatty in a much different light. Montag suddenly sees that, although he always assumed that all firemen were happy, he has no right to make this assumption any longer. Although Beatty seemed the most severe critic of books, he, in fact, thought that outlawing individual thinking and putting a premium on conformity stifled a society. Beatty was a man who understood his own compromised morality and who privately admired the conviction of people like Montag.

In a strange way, Beatty wanted to commit suicide but was evidently too cowardly to carry it out. Bradbury illustrates the general unhappiness and despondency of certain members of society three times before Beatty's incident: Millie's near-suicide with the overdose of sleeping pills; the oblique reference to the fireman in Seattle, who "purposely set a Mechanical Hound to his own chemical complex and let it loose"; and the unidentified woman who chose immolation along with her books. People in Montag's society are simply not happy. Their desire for death reflects a social malaise of meaningless and purposelessness.

When war is finally declared, the hint of doom, which has been looming on the horizon during the entire novel, now reaches a climax. This new development serves as another parallel to the situation in which Montag finds himself. Montag sees his former life fall apart as the city around him faces a battle in which it will also be destroyed.

As Montag runs, his wounded leg feels like a "chunk of burnt pine log" that he is forced to carry "as a penance for some obscure sin." Again, the imagery of fire is used to suggest purification. The penance Montag must pay is the result of all his years of destruction as a fireman. Even though the pain in his leg is excruciating, he must overcome even more daunting obstacles before he achieves redemption.

Unexpectedly, the seemingly simple task of crossing the boulevard proves to be his next obstacle. The "beetles" travel at such high speeds that they are likened to bullets fired from invisible rifles. Bradbury enlists fire imagery to describe these beetles: Their headlights seem to burn Montag's cheeks, and as one of their lights bears down on him, it seems like "a torch hurtling upon him."

After Montag and Faber make their plans for escape, the reader witnesses Faber's devotion to the plans that he and Montag have made. In choosing to flee to St. Louis to find an old printer friend, Faber also places his life in jeopardy to ensure the immortality of books.

Montag imagines his manhunt as a "game," then as a "circus" that "must go on," and finally as a "one-man carnival." Montag's thoughts, however, do not mean that he imagines it as something silly or playful, but instead, in his community, he considers everyday experience to be a spectacle.

When Montag escapes to the river, the imagery of water, a traditional symbol of regeneration and renewal (and, for Carl Jung, transformation), coupled with Montag's dressing in Faber's clothes, suggests that Montag's tale of transformation is complete. He has shed his past life and is now a new person with a new meaning in life.

His time spent in the water, accompanied by the escape from the city, serves as an epiphany for Montag's spirit: "For the first time in a dozen years [that is, since he became a fireman] the stars were coming out above him, in great processions of wheeling fire." The escape allows Montag — again, for the first time in years — to think. He thinks about his dual roles as man and fireman. "After a long time of floating on the land and a short time of floating in the river," the reader is told, "he knew why he must never burn again in his life." Only human beings are capable of making choices (and, hence, are capable of being moral), and his moral choice is to cease burning.

While floating in the river, Montag suddenly realizes the change that has taken place: "He felt as if he had left a stage behind him and many actors... He was moving from an unreality that was frightening into a reality that was unreal because it was new." Montag recognizes that many people, including himself and Beatty, were forced to play an assigned role in their lives. The stage imagery implies that Montag actually realized that he was merely acting for a long period of his life, and that he is now entering into an entirely new stage of life.

Montag emerges from the river transformed. Now in the country, his first tangible sensation — "the dry smell of hay blowing from some distant field" — stirs strong melancholic emotions. Though Montag may be a man who has trouble articulating his feelings, one learns that he is a man of deep emotions. The entire episode of him leaving the river and entering the countryside is evocative of a spiritual transformation. He has sad thoughts of Millie, who is somewhere back in the city, and has a sensuous fantasy of Clarisse; both of which are now associated with the city and a life that he no longer lives, to which he can never return.

Whereas the city was metaphorically associated with a stifling and oppressive technology, the countryside is a place of unbounded possibility, which at first terrifies Montag: "He was crushed by darkness and the look of the country and the million odors on a wind that iced the body." In his earlier life, recall that Montag could smell only kerosene, which was "nothing but perfume" to him. The forest into which he stumbles is rampant with life; he imagines "a billion leaves on the land" and is overcome by the natural odors that confront him.

To underscore the strangeness of this new environment, Bradbury makes Montag stumble across a railroad track that had, for Montag, "a familiarity." He is, ironically, more familiar with an environment composed of concrete and steel than he is with grass and trees. Because he is most familiar (and comfortable) with something associated with urban life (the railroad tracks), Montag remembers that Faber told him to follow them — "the single familiar thing, the magic charm he might need a little while, to touch, to feel beneath his feet" — as he moves on.

When he sees the fire in the distance, the reader sees the profound change that Montag has undergone. Montag sees the fire as "strange," because "It was burning, it was *warming*." This fire doesn't destroy but heals, and by doing so, it draws Montag to the company of his fellow outcasts, book burners of a different sort.

Curiously, Granger was expecting Montag, and when he offers him "a small bottle of colorless fluid," Montag takes his final step toward transformation. Not only is Montag garbed in clothes that are not his, but the chemical that Granger offers him changes his perspiration. Literally, Montag becomes a different man.

When Montag expresses his prior knowledge of the Book of Ecclesiastes, Granger is happy to tell Montag of his new purpose in life: Montag will become that book. Not only does Montag learn the value of a book, but he also learns that he can "become the book."

Talking with Granger and the others around the fire, Montag gains a sense of warmth and personal well-being and recovers a sense of faith in the future. He begins gaining an understanding of the fire of spirit, life, and immortality, as well as forgetting the fire that destroys. Notice that when the campfire is no longer necessary, every man lends a hand to help put it out. ("We are model citizens, in our own special way," Granger says.) This action is further proof of the things that Granger has been telling Montag: Group effort is necessary if a positive goal is ever to be reached.

When the commune moves south (due to the war threat), Montag associates Millie with the city, but he admits to Granger that, strangely, he doesn't "feel much of anything" for her. That part of his life, as well as everything relating to the city, seems distant and unreal. He feels sorry for her because he intuitively knows that she will probably be killed in the war. He is also ashamed, because in all their years together, he was able to offer her nothing.

As the city is destroyed ("as quick as the whisper of a scythe the war was finished"), Montag's thoughts return to Millie. He imagines how the last moments of her life must have been. He pictures her looking at her wall television set. Suddenly, the television screen goes blank, and Millie is left seeing only a mirror image of herself. Montag imagines that just before her death, Millie finally sees and knows for herself how superficial and empty her life has been. And, in that instant, Montag recalls when he met her: "A long time ago" in Chicago. His former life seems like only a dream.

A new day begins, and a fire providing the commune warmth and heat for cooking is made. Granger looks into the fire and realizes its life-giving quality as he utters the word "phoenix." The phoenix, he says, was "a silly damn bird" that "every few hundred years" built a pyre "and burned himself up." Granger imagines the bird as "first cousin to Man" because the bird continually went through rebirth only to destroy himself again. The mythology of fire surrounding this ancient bird is strategic to the lessons of *Fahrenheit 451.*

Bradbury alludes to the phoenix repeatedly in the novel. The firemen wear an emblem of the phoenix on their chests; Beatty wears the sign of the phoenix on his hat and drives a phoenix car. When Beatty is burned to death, his death by fire prepares for a rebirth that the phoenix sign traditionally symbolizes. Montag's destruction of Beatty ultimately results in his escape from the city and his meeting with Granger. All of these actions lead to a rebirth of a new and vital life. Montag's new life is filled with hope and the promise of a new era of humanism, depicted in the words that Montag recalls from the Bible: "To everything there is a season. A time to break down, a time to build up."

With Granger leading the way, the commune heads toward the city to help those who may need them. It is a curious moment, but characteristic of Bradbury. In his novel *The Martian Chronicles*, for example, people flee the Earth and head for Mars because they are sure that Earth is going to be destroyed in a nuclear holocaust. However, when the transplanted Earth people hear that the holocaust has occurred, they return to Earth immediately because they know that it no longer exists as they remember it. This movement is repeated at the conclusion of *Fahrenheit 451*. Montag flees the city only to return after its destruction. Although altruistically compelled to lend aid to the survivors (of which there were very few), Montag (and the others) seems to have some ritualistic need to return to the city from which they escaped. Even though they escaped the city for political reasons, its familiarity nonetheless remains psychologically comforting. The implication is that, in the death of someone or something that you fiercely hate, you also loose an essential part of your identity.

Fahrenheit 451 is explicit in its warnings and moral lessons aimed at the present. Bradbury believes that human social organization can easily become oppressive and regimented unless it changes its present course of suppression of an individual's innate rights through censorship. The degenerated future depicted in *Fahrenheit 451* represents the culmination of dangerous tendencies that are submerged in your own society. At the very least, the book asserts that the freedom of imagination is a corollary of individual freedom.

The title that Bradbury gives to Part Three alludes to William Blake's poem "The Tyger." Many interpret this poem, from Blake's *Songs of Innocence and Experience*, as a meditation about the origin of evil in the world. The first four lines of the poem are:

Tyger, Tyger burning bright,

In the forests of the night:

What immortal hand or eye,

Could frame thy fearful symmetry?

In Blake's poem, the tiger is often considered a symbol for a world in which evil is at work; it speaks also of the dual nature of all existence. Appropriately, Part Three's title, "Burning Bright," serves a dual function: It summarizes the situation at the conclusion of the book. Even while the city burns brightly from the war's destruction, the spirit of the commune also brightly burns, signifying a future of hope and optimism.

Glossary

Burning Bright the heading derives from "The Tyger," a poem by William Blake.

Icarus the son of Daedalus; escaping from Crete by flying with wings made of Daedalus, Icarus flies so high that the sun's heat melts the wax by which his wings are fastened, and he falls to his death in the sea. Beatty alludes to Icarus with the comment: "Old Montag wanted to fly near the sun and now that he's burnt his damn wings, he wonders why."

You think you can walk on water Beatty alludes to Jesus walking on water, as recorded in Mark 6:45-51.

There is no terror, Cassius, in your threats, for I am arm'd so strong in honesty that they pass by me as an idle wind, which I respect not Beattytaunts Montag with a passage from Shakespeare's *Julius Caesar*, Act IV, Scene iii, Line 66.

there's lots of old Harvard degrees on the tracks Faber refers to the educated people who have dropped out of sight to live the hobo life outside the city.

Keystone Comedy from 1914 to 1920, director Mack Sennett and Keystone Studios produced a series of madcap silent film comedies featuring the Keystone Cops.

the guild of the asbestos-weaver Montag associates his desire to stop the burning with the formation of a new trade union. Like the guilds of the Middle Ages, the asbestos-weavers symbolize progress against the tyranny of the past.

coat of a thousand colors Granger alludes to Joseph, the character in Genesis 37:3-4 who receives a long-sleeved, ornamental coat of many colors from Jacob, his doting father. The coat, symbolizing favoritism shown by Jacob toward his son, alienates the other sons, who sell their brother to passing traders, stain the coat with goat's blood, and return it to their father to prove that a wild animal has eaten Joseph.

crying in the wilderness Granger compares his group's minority status to John the Baptist, the prophet whom Isaiah predicted would one day announce the coming of the Messiah (Isaiah 40: 3-5).

V-2 rocket the German's use of the first long-range, liquid-fuel missile carrying a ton of explosives during World War II changed the face of modern warfare.

atom-bomb mushroom on August 6, 1945, over Hiroshima, Japan, American pilots dropped the first atomic bomb used in the war. The explosion, which rose in a straight column two hundred miles high, ballooned outward like a huge mushroom.

I hate a Roman named Status Quo! Granger's grandfather made a pun out of the Latin phrase, which means the situation as it now exists.

whisper of a scythe an extended metaphor begins with a giant hand sowing the grains of bombs over the land. The image concludes with the death-dealing scythe, the symbol carried in the hand of Father Time, an image of death, which cuts down life in a single, silent sweep.

To everything there is a season Montag recalls an often-quoted segment of Ecclesiastes 3:1-8, which reminds him that there is a time for dying as well as a time for living.

And on either side of the river was there a tree of life, which bore twelve manner of fruits, and yielded her fruit every month; and the leaves of the tree are for the healing of the nations a prophecy from verse two of Revelation 22, the last book in the Bible.

CHARACTER ANALYSIS

Guy Montag

The novel's protagonist, Guy Montag, takes pride in his work with the fire department. A third-generation fireman, Montag fits the stereotypical role, with his "black hair, black brows...fiery face, and...blue-steel shaved but unshaved look." Montag takes great joy in his work and serves as a model of twenty-fourth-century professionalism. Reeking of cinders and ash, he enjoys dressing in his uniform, playing the role of a symphony conductor as he directs the brass nozzle toward illegal books, and smelling the kerosene that raises the temperature to the required 451 degrees Fahrenheit — the temperature at which book paper ignites. In his first eight years of employment, Montag even joined in the firemen's bestial sport of letting small animals loose and betting on which ones the Mechanical Hound would annihilate first.

In the last two years, however, a growing discontent has grown in Montag, a "fireman turned sour" who cannot yet name the cause of his emptiness and disaffection. He characterizes his restless mind as "full of bits and pieces," and he requires sedatives to sleep. His hands, more attuned to his inner workings than his conscious mind, seem to take charge of his behavior. Daily, he returns to a loveless, meaningless marriage symbolized by his cold bedroom furnished with twin beds. Drawn to the lights and conversation of the McClellan family next door, he forces himself to remain at home, yet he watches them through the French windows.

Through his friendship with Clarisse McClellan, Montag perceives the harshness of society as opposed to the joys of nature in which he rarely partakes. When Clarisse teases him about not being in love, he experiences an epiphany and sinks into a despair that characterizes most of the novel. He suffers guilt for hiding books behind the hall ventilator grille and for failing to love his wife, whom he cannot remember meeting for the first time. But even though he harbors no affection for Mildred, Montag shudders at the impersonal, mechanized medical care that restores his dying wife to health.

Montag's moroseness reaches a critical point after he witnesses the burning of an old woman, who willingly embraces death when the firemen come to burn her books. His psychosomatic illness, a significant mix of chills and fever, fails to fool his employer, who easily identifies the cause of Montag's malaise — a dangerously expanded sensibility in a world that prizes a dulled consciousness. Lured by books, Montag forces Mildred to join him in reading. His hunger for humanistic knowledge drives him to Professor Faber, the one educated person that he can trust to teach him.

Following the burning of the old woman, his company's first human victim, Montag faces an agonizing spiritual dilemma of love and hate for his job. As a fireman, he is marked by the phoenix symbol, but ironically, he is inhibited from rising like the fabled bird because he lacks the know-how to transform intellectual growth into deeds. After he contacts Faber, however, Montag begins a metamorphosis that signifies his rebirth as the phoenix of a new generation. A duality evolves, the blend of himself and Faber, his alter ego. With Faber's help, Montag weathers the transformation and returns to his job to confront Captain Beatty, his nemesis. Beatty classifies Montag's problem as an intense romanticism actualized by his contact with Clarisse. Pulled back and forth between Faber's words from the listening device in his ear and the cynical sneers and gibes of Beatty, who cites lines from so many works of literature that he dazzles his adversary, Montag moves blindly to the fire truck when an alarm sounds. Beatty, who rarely drives, takes the wheel and propels the fire truck toward the next target — Montag's house.

When Beatty prepares to arrest him, Montag realizes that he cannot contain his loathing for a sadistic, escapist society. Momentarily contemplating the consequences of his act, he ignites Beatty and watches him burn. As Montag races away from the lurid scene, he momentarily suffers a wave of remorse but quickly concludes that Beatty maneuvered him into the killing. Resourceful and courageous, Montag outwits the Mechanical Hound, but impaired by a numbed leg, he is nearly run over by a car full of murderous teenage joyriders. With Faber's help, he embraces his budding idealism and hopes for escaping to a better life, one in which dissent and discussion redeem humanity from its gloomy dark age.

Baptized to a new life by his plunge into the river and dressed in Faber's clothes, Montag flees the cruel society, which is fated to suffer a brief, annihilating attack. The cataclysm forces him face down onto the earth, where he experiences a disjointed remembrance of his courtship ten years earlier. Just as his leg recovers its feeling, Montag's humanity returns. After Granger helps him accept the destruction of the city and the probable annihilation of Mildred, Montag looks forward to a time when people and books can again flourish.

Captain Beatty

A satanic presence enshrouded in "thunderheads of tobacco smoke," Captain Beatty is the shrewd, ruthless antagonist of the story; he is linked repeatedly to fire (which ultimately kills him) and to the Fates as represented by recurrent card games. As leader of a fire company, he hosts an unwholesome camaraderie with the bureaucratized book burners who follow his orders. Symbolically, he drives a "yellow-flame-colored beetle with...black, char-colored tires." Like the Mechanical Hound, he noses out information, such as the pattern of disloyalty in firemen, Montag's relationship with Clarisse, and the presence of books in Montag's house. He remains attuned to the idiosyncrasies of his men and is not deceived by Montag's feigned illness. His authoritarian nature surfaces in his terse order to Mildred to turn off her screens and to Guy to return to work later in the shift.

A malicious, destructive phoenix fire chief, Beatty is an educated, perceptive manipulator who surrounds himself with a nest of literary snippets. From this mishmash of aphorisms, he selects appropriate weapons with which to needle and vex Montag, his adversary, in a one-sided verbal duel. Beatty's stand against the dissenting fireman is an essential outgrowth of his role as the sole phoenix in this dark world. At Montag's bedside and later in front of his house, Beatty overestimates his control of a desperate man. When Montag sets him aflame (somewhat encouraged by Beatty), Beatty burns into black ash, opening the way for Montag to spring into his own incarnation as the succeeding phoenix and bringer of light.

Clarisse McClellan

A lover of life and nature, Clarisse, an affable neighbor who is seventeen, is the foil of Mildred — Montag's cold, mindless, conforming wife. Delightfully human and aware of her surroundings, Clarisse disdains the fact-learning that passes for modern education. She enjoys rain, dandelions, autumn leaves, and even sessions with her analyst, who misdiagnosis her exuberance for living.

Powered by an insatiable curiosity, Clarisse, whom Beatty labels a "time bomb," serves as the catalyst that impels Montag toward a painful but necessary self-examination. With gentle pricks to his self-awareness, Clarisse reveals to him the absence of love, pleasure, and contentment in his life. Her role in the novel is only the forerunner of the spiritual revitalization completed by Faber and Granger. Her terrible death, nearly repeated when a careening vehicle passes over the tip of Montag's finger, underscores the rampant dehumanization of society and the resulting random acts of violence.

Professor Faber

Quivering on the brink of rebellion against the causal drift of society from humanism to oppression, Professor Faber, a bloodless, white-haired academic who protects his "peanut-brittle bones" and castigates himself for his "terrible cowardice," represents a sterling redeeming quality — a belief in the integrity of the individual. He reveres the magic in literature, which "stitched the patches of the universe into one garment for us."

Because he is over twice Montag's age and was forced into exile forty years earlier, Faber provides the look backward that enables the hero to see how a literate society allowed itself to slide into mechanization and repression. Willing to read books, discuss philosophies, and enable his disciple to escape the avenging dystopia, Faber is reduced to a soothing, insightful, cajoling voice (serving as Montag's conscience) in Montag's ear. However, Faber is invigorated by his contact with Montag, and after the listening device falls into Beatty's hands, he leaves the disintegrating city for St. Louis, where he hopes to produce books with a fellow bibliophile.

Mildred Montag

Montag's wife whom he courted in Chicago and married when they both were twenty, Mildred characterizes shallowness and mediocrity. Her abnormally white flesh and chemically burnt hair epitomize a society that demands an artificial beauty in women through diets and hair dye. Completely immersed in an electronic world and growing more incompatible with Montag with every electronic gadget that enters her house, she fills her waking hours with manic drives in the beetle and by watching a TV clown, who distracts her from her real feelings and leads her nearly to suicide from a drug overdose. Unwilling and unable to analyze rationally, she lives the shallow life that Beatty touts — acquiescence to a technological chamber of horrors. She distances herself from real emotion by identifying with "the family," a three-dimensional fiction in which she plays a scripted part. Her longing for a fourth wall of television suggests her capability of submerging in fantasy to withdraw from the roles of wife, mother, and whole human being.

Addicted to the labor-saving machines that toast and butter her bread and fill her mind with simplistic entertainment, she forgets to bring aspirin to her ailing husband and recedes into monosyllabic communication. Her replies to him are impersonal and callous, as illustrated by her bland announcement of Clarisse's death. To remove any doubts about her materialistic, robotic lifestyle, Mildred surrounds herself with friends like Clara Phelps and Ann Bowles, vapid and witless dullards who select a presidential candidate by his televised good looks. Unsurprisingly, Mildred betrays her husband and flees their marriage while mourning the loss of her TV family. Her white-powdered face, her colorless lips, and her stiff body foreshadow the corpse she soon becomes. The oppression and militarism that she so willingly accepts expectedly turns on her and exterminates her in a single apocalyptic blast.

Granger

The foil of Captain Beatty, Granger is also associated with burning. However, the warming, beneficial campfire surrounded by his coterie of book people contrasts with the malicious, doom-filled conflagrations set by Beatty. Granger is the author of *The Fingers in the Glove: The Proper Relationship between the Individual and Society*, a capsule statement of Bradbury's theme. Granger's pragmatic, uplifting words lead Montag from flight to the safety of the forest.

In contrast to Beatty and his Hound, Granger applies his own technological wizardry. To defeat the trail-sniffing Hound, he offers the scent of a bobcat to dissociate Montag from his former odor by applying a safer olfactory identity. Granger represents the balance that has reentered the world and which will alleviate the dark age with a new spark of intellectual light. He reveres his grandfather, a sculptor, for the humanistic spark he left behind. With cities lying in charred heaps at his back, Granger, a twenty-fourth-century Moses, guides his fellow rescuers of books toward an undisclosed promised land.

The Mechanical Hound

A reincarnation of the vengeful Furies from Greek mythology and the epitome of modern perverted science, the Mechanical Hound is a slick electronic hit man formed of copper wire and storage batteries and smelling of blue electricity. He is an omnipresent menace capable of storing "so many amino acids, so much sulphur, so much butterfat and alkaline" that he can inexorably trail the odor index of ten thousand victims to their doom. From his snout projects a "four-inch hollow steel needle," which can inject enough morphine or procaine to quell a rat, cat, or chicken within three seconds. Sniffing its quarry with "sensitive capillary hairs in the Nylon-brushed nostrils," the Hound growls and then scuttles silently toward its prey on eight rubber-padded feet. Sighting through the "green-blue neon light" of its multifaceted eyes, the Hound is masterminded by a central command for rapid deployment and near perfect accuracy.

The Hound represents government control and manipulation of technology. Originally, dogs served as the rescuers for firemen. They were given the job of sniffing out the injured or weak. However, in this dystopia, the Hound has been made into a watchdog of society. Like the Furies, the Mechanical Hound has been programmed (by the government) to avenge and punish citizens who break society's rules. The ones who are not loyal to the rules must especially be punished, and the Hound serves as the enforcer of these rules.

CRITICAL ESSAYS

Dystopian Fiction and *Fahrenheit 451*

When examining *Fahrenheit 451* as a piece of dystopian fiction, a definition for the term "dystopia" is required. *Dystopia* is often used as an antonym of "utopia," a perfect world often imagined existing in the future. A dystopia, therefore, is a terrible place. You may find it more helpful (and also more accurate) to conceive a dystopian literary tradition, a literary tradition that's created worlds containing reactions against certain ominous social trends and therefore imagines a disastrous future if these trends are not reversed. Most commonly cited as the model of a twentieth-century dystopian novel is Yevgeny Zamiatin's *We* (1924), which envisions an oppressive but stable social order accomplished only through the complete effacement of the individual. *We*, which may more properly be called an anti-utopian work rather than a dystopian work, is often cited as the precursor of George Orwell's *1984* (1948), a nightmarish vision of a totalitarian world of the future, similar to one portrayed in *We*, in which terrorist force maintains order.

We and *1984* are often cited as classic dystopian fictions, along with Aldous Huxley's *Brave New World* (1932), which, contrary to popular belief, has a somewhat different purpose and object of attack than the previously mentioned novels. Huxley's *Brave New World* has as its target representations of a blind faith in the idea of social and technological progress.

In contrast to dystopian novels like Huxley's and Orwell's, however, Bradbury's *Fahrenheit 451* does not picture villainous dictators (like Orwell's O'Brien) or corrupt philosopher-kings (like Huxley's Mustapha Mond), although Bradbury's Captain Beatty shares a slight similarity to Mustapha Mond. The crucial difference is that Bradbury's novel does not focus on a ruling elite nor does it portray a higher society, but rather, it portrays the means of oppression and regimentation through the life of an uneducated and complacent, though an ultimately honest and virtuous, working-class hero (Montag). In contrast, Orwell and Huxley choose to portray the lives of petty bureaucrats (Winston Smith and Bernard Marx, respectively), whose alienated lives share similarities to the literary characters of author Franz Kafka (1883-1924).

Nonetheless, points of similarity exist between these works. All three imagine a technocratic social order maintained through oppression and regimentation and by the complete effacement of the individual. All these authors envision a populace distracted by the pursuit of explicit images, which has the effect of creating politically enervated individuals.

Huxley envisions a World State in which war has been eradicated in order to achieve social stability; Bradbury and Orwell imagine that war itself achieves the same end — by keeping the populace cowering in fear of an enemy attack, whether the enemy is real or not. The war maintains the status quo because any change in leaders may topple the defense structure. Orwell and Bradbury imagine the political usefulness of the anesthetization of experience: All experiences become form without substance. The populace is not able to comprehend that all they do is significant and has meaning Likewise, Bradbury and Huxley imagine the use of chemical sedatives and tranquilizers as a means of compensating for an individual's alienated existence. More importantly, all three authors imagine a technocratic social order accomplished through the suppression of books — that is, through *censorship.*

However, despite their similarities, you can also draw a crucial distinction between these books. If the failure of the *proles* (citizens of the lowest class; workers) reveals Orwell's despair at the British working-class political consciousness, and if Mustapha Mond reveals Huxley's cynical view of the intellectual, Guy Montag's personal victory over the government system represents American optimism. This train of thought leads back to Henry David Thoreau, whose *Civil Disobedience* Bradbury must hold in high esteem. Recall the remark by Juan Ramon Jimenez that serves as an epigraph to *Fahrenheit 451*: "If they give you ruled paper, write the other way." This epigraph could have easily served as Thoreau's motto and is proof of Bradbury's interest in individual freedom. Bradbury's trust in the virtue of the individual and his belief in the inherently corrupt nature of government is a central concept of *Fahrenheit 451.*

Continuing Bradbury's inspection of personal freedom in *Fahrenheit 451*, you must first examine the freedoms that the author gives to the characters. As mentioned previously, you know that all sense of past was obliterated by the entrance of technology (the TV characters give citizens the opportunity to create a past and present through their story lines). Likewise, through the use of TV, individuals do not understand the importance of the past in their own lives. They have been repeatedly given propaganda about the past, so they have no reason to question its authenticity or value.

Also, because of the technology the characters are given, no one (of course, except for Faber, Granger, Clarisse, and eventually Montag) understands the value of books in direct relation to their own personal development. Television, for the majority of individuals in *Fahrenheit 451*, does not create conflicting sentiments or cause people to think, so why would they welcome challenge? As Millie points out to Montag, "Books aren't people. You read and I look all around, but there isn't *anybody*! . . . My 'family' is people. They tell me things: I laugh, they laugh. . . ."

Because the majority of this dystopian society is not able to express personal freedom, it is interesting that Clarisse and the unidentified old woman die early in the novel in order to display what has happened so far in this society to the people who exercise their personal freedom. It's also important to see that even Millie, who serves as the model of this society's conformity, almost dies as a result of her one act of personal rebellion when she attempts suicide. Likewise, perhaps even Captain Beatty's demise is an act of personal freedom because Beatty goads Montag into killing him instead of protecting himself and remaining alive.

The battle of having personal freedom is essential in this book because Bradbury demonstrates what happens when man is not given the opportunity to express his thoughts or remember his past. Through Clarisse, the unidentified woman, Millie, and Beatty, you are shown the consequences of what happens when humans aren't allowed to fully express their individuality and choice (they die). Through the characters of Montag, Faber, and Granger, you can see how one individual can make a difference in society if that one individual can fully realize the importance of his or her past, as well as be willing to fight for the opportunity to express himself or herself.

The Issue of Censorship and *Fahrenheit 451*

Bradbury ties personal freedom to the right of an individual having the freedom of expression when he utilizes the issue of censorship in *Fahrenheit 451*. The First Amendment to the United States Constitution reads:

Congress shall make no law respecting an establishment of religion, or prohibiting the free exercise thereof; or abridging the freedom of speech or of the press; or the right of the people peaceably to assemble, and to petition the government for redress of grievances.

The common reading of the First Amendment is that commitment to free speech is not the acceptance of only non-controversial expressions that enjoy general approval. To accept a commitment to the First Amendment means, in the words of Justice Holmes, "freedom for what we hate." As quoted in Students' Right to Read (NCTE, 1982), "Censorship leaves students with an inadequate and distorted picture of the ideals, values, and problems of their culture. Writers may often be the spokesmen of their culture, or they may stand to the side, attempting to describe and evaluate that culture. Yet, partly because of censorship or the fear of censorship, many writers are ignored or inadequately represented in the public schools, and many are represented in anthologies not by their best work but by their safest or least offensive work." What are the issues involved in censorship?

Imagine that a group wants to ban *Fahrenheit 451* because Montag defies authority. For the sake of the argument, assume for a moment that you wish to "ban" *Fahrenheit 451* from the library shelves. To do so, you must do a number of things. First, you must establish why defying authority is wrong. What are its consequences? What are the probable effects on youth to see flagrant disregard of authority? (In regard to these questions, you may want to read Plato's *Apology* to get a sense of how to argue the position.) Second, you must have some theory of psychology, either implied or directly stated. That is, you must establish how a reading of *Fahrenheit 451* would inspire a student to flagrantly disregard authority. Why is reading bad for a student? How can it be bad? Next, you must establish how a student who reads *Fahrenheit 451* will read the book and extract from it a message that says "Defy Authority Whenever Possible" and then act on this message.

You must then reconcile whatever argument you construct with the responsibilities that accompany accepting the rights of the First Amendment.

Perhaps you should consider and think about the issues of free speech and fundamental rights that you may not have considered before. Indeed, you may conclude that you can't claim your own right to expression if you have the right to suppress others rights to express themselves.

In looking at censorship in *Fahrenheit 451*, Bradbury sends a very direct message showing readers what can happen if they allow the government to take total control of what they do (or do not) read, watch, and discuss. For example, the government in *Fahrenheit 451* has taken control and demanded that books be given the harshest measure of censorship — systematic destruction by burning.

Although the books and people have fallen victims to censorship in *Fahrenheit 451*, luckily, some citizens remain who are willing to sacrifice their lives to ensure that books remain alive. As Faber notes in a conversation with Montag, "It's not books you need, it's some of the things that once were in books." Faber then continues this conversation with Montag pointing out that people need "the right to carry out actions based on what we learn [from books]. . . ."

Because the government has censored so much in its society, the citizens in *Fahrenheit 451* have no idea about what is truly happening in their world. A direct result of their limited knowledge is that their entire city is destroyed because propaganda wouldn't allow individuals to see that their destruction was imminent.

Comparison of the Book and Film Versions of *Fahrenheit 451*

All these themes, dystopian society, censorship, and freedom of the individual, are addressed in the 1967 Vineyard Films' (Universal) version of *Fahrenheit 451*. Although the film reiterates the themes and basis of the book, there are many differences to contrast.

In examining the film and novel, one important item to note is that the same actress, Julie Christie, plays both Linda (Mildred's name in the film) and Clarisse. When looking at this casting decision, one can deduce that the film director, Frances Truffault, purposefully made this decision to show the audience that the women are similar in the way that they cannot continue as they are in the present society. Although the two women are dramatically different in their beliefs, Montag continually searches for signs of Clarisse's energy and enthusiasm in his wife. Montag, is not focusing upon their physical appearance; he's instead trying to find the internal wisdom and soul of the two women that he sees.

Unfortunately, Clarisse dies in the book when Montag begins to understand her. However, in the film, Clarisse survives and, in fact, becomes his teacher (she, in a way, replaces the character of Faber from the book who doesn't appear in the film). She is the character who guides Montag to the book people hiding in the woods outside the city.

Contemplate the fact that in the book, no women are present at the end of the novel, but in the film, women play a role in the reconstruction of the new society. Possibly, this difference reflects that the book was written in 1953, whereas the film was made 14 years later.

Regardless of the differences between the film and the book upon which the film is based, both stories of *Fahrenheit 451* tackle the issues of a society that has allowed its government to take total control. Chillingly, people in this society have forgotten their histories and have allowed themselves to become victims of propaganda and censorship. In following the protagonist, Guy Montag, through his struggle and rebirth, the reader (and viewer) are given the opportunity to see that the human spirit triumphs and that the important knowledge that books can impart will never be destroyed.

Ray Bradbury's Fiction

Introduction

Calling Ray Bradbury a "science fiction author" (which is an inaccurate label) is commonplace. In fact, to pigeonhole his writings as "science fiction" obscures rather than clarifies Bradbury's work. The reader may find it useful to take a brief overview of Bradbury's fiction in order to sort out the various types of fiction that he writes, as well as consider various ways of understanding his work, rather that lumping it fallaciously into the narrow category of science fiction.

Beyond Science Fiction

The perceptive critic Peter Nicholls, writing in the *Science Fiction Encyclopedia* (Doubleday, 1979), is reluctant to place Bradbury's work in the science fiction genre. On the contrary, he finds Bradbury's themes "traditionally American" and says that Bradbury's choosing "to render them [his themes] on several important occasions in sf [science fiction] imagery does not make RB [Ray Bradbury] a sf writer, even though his early years were devoted to the form." Nicholls concludes that Bradbury is, in fact, a "whimsical fantasist in an older tradition."

Humanist Gilbert Highet, in his "Introduction" to *The Vintage Bradbury* (Vintage, 1965), agrees with Nicholls. He finds Bradbury to have such illustrious European predecessors as Villiers de l'Isle-Adam (1840-1889), E.T.A. Hoffman (1776-1822), H.G. Wells (1866-1946), and (Joseph) Rudyard Kipling (1865-1936). Early American fantasists include Edgar Allan Poe (1809-1849), Ambrose Bierce (1842-1914), H.P. Lovecraft (1890-1937), and Charles G. Finney (1905-1984). In fact, Finney's *Circus of Dr. Lao* (1935) was a major influence on Bradbury's works. Note, too, that the only science fiction writers whom Bradbury consistently mentions are those whom he considers his "teachers' — Leigh Brackett and Henry Kuttner.

The literary critic and writer J.B. Priestley has observed that despite the fact that Bradbury is often identified as a science fiction writer, Bradbury "is concerned not with gadgets but with men's feelings. He creates imaginatively, and it may be assumed that he's not merely turning out stuff for a new and flourishing [science fiction] market but is trying to express some of his own deepest feelings." Priestley goes on to suggest that behind all of Bradbury's tales are "deep feelings of anxiety, fear, and guilt."

Bradbury's characters are earnest in their quest for a way in which they can effectively deal with the problem of evil. They are hungry to know who they are and how they can achieve their full potential, and yet, simultaneously, these same brave human beings are terribly afraid of growing old and dying.

As a result of the themes with which Bradbury consistently works, his texts often take on a strongly evangelical tone, because he always insists that the only hope for the world lies within the individual. "I realize very late in life now that I could have made a fine priest or minister," confesses Bradbury. The truth of this claim lies in Bradbury's exposing humanity for what it is while offering moral encouragement by showing humans what they can be. That is, Bradbury attempts to present humankind with a vision of the best possible of all worlds — a utopia. And for Bradbury, this utopia is attainable. Furthermore, Bradbury's philosophical idealism insists that once humans discover and attain this utopia within themselves, their universe accordingly improves. However, before humankind can achieve Bradbury's utopia, it must first conquer, or at least learn to cope adequately, with the evil that confronts it at every hour with feelings of loneliness and unfulfillment. This "evil" is usually the inability of humans to know themselves fully, the fear of growing old, and the fear of death.

Use of Imagery

The focus on death is threaded throughout Bradbury's writings, and alongside death is Bradbury's deep interest in the themes of deceit, dissatisfaction with the self, the reality of evil and how to contend with it, and the attainment of self-knowledge. As one may expect, these concepts are embodied in traditional images: ravine imagery, mirror imagery, water imagery, carnival imagery, sun and fire imagery, and the opposition of light and dark, good and evil.

In particular, both the physical and psychological aspects of death and dying are examined through Bradbury's use of ravine imagery. A ravine (defined as a long, deep hollow in the earth's surface, especially one worn by the action of a stream) is used to show that like life, many of the things that exist on this Earth change. Bradbury believes that if we can face and understand our own individual, ultimate deaths, then we can appreciate ourselves and our lives to a fuller degree. He believes that it's necessary to "meet and know and chew and swallow death as a writer and as a reader" and to exorcise it from the subconscious so that we will not have to think about it all the time. Only then can we continue with our real business — which is living.

Frequently, Bradbury also uses imagery associated with masks. Masks, of course, are often associated with deceit, deception, and games. To put on a mask is to be able to mimic, but if we put on a mask, we permit ourselves to disguise our feelings. Therefore, in Bradbury's works, a mask is always an attractive but a dangerous element.

Mirror imagery in Bradbury's stories frequently illustrates the theme of dissatisfaction with ourselves. In some instances, too, Bradbury employs mirror imagery as an emblem of reality, depicting our fascination with what mirrors tell us about ourselves. However, mention of this mirror imagery is not complete without also mentioning the antithesis of reality — that is, fantasy. Bradbury's mirror also allows us to envision ourselves in all the splendor that we wish to see ourselves as well as how we wish to be seen by others. Also inherent in any analysis of mirror imagery is Bradbury's conservative view that we are only who we are, and any attempt at altering ourselves can lead only to disaster.

Bradbury's carnival imagery is a vivid device that he often uses to effectively focus on the presence of evil as a real force in the world. A study of his carnival imagery reveals his belief that the potential for evil exists in a dormant form in each of us. That is, Bradbury believes that unless we keep that which is good within us in fit condition by actively exercising it, we will lose our ability to combat evil, thus allowing evil to grow and become powerful.

The battle between good and evil appears in several images contained in Bradbury's works. One such image is the sun, which functions symbolically as a source of life and also as a symbol for the wholeness of humankind. Very simply, for Bradbury, light is good and dark is evil.

However, a number of Bradbury's stories go a step further, using sun imagery as a symbol for God and the promise of immortality. Similarly, Bradbury's fire imagery focuses on the theme of the victory of good over evil. Appropriately, Bradbury's fire imagery and his sun imagery function hand-in-hand, because one can symbolically consider fire as the sun's earthly representative. The works that deal most specifically with fire imagery contain Bradbury's most important social commentaries concerning the condition of the world as he sees it. His most intense pleas in favor of the arts and humanities, as opposed to sterile technology, occur in stories that use sun and fire imagery.

Another image that Bradbury often uses to show the possibilities for overcoming evil in the world is the smile. Smiles and laughter, according to Bradbury, derive their power from their forefather — love. Bradbury believes that love is the strongest and most humanizing force that man possesses.

Our knowledge of death as a part of life, our learning to make the best of who and what we are, our acceptance of evil as well as good in the world, and our battle to arrest evil are the discoveries that give us a broader insight into ourselves.

Bradbury also presents this self-knowledge in his stories through the use of water imagery. Bradbury uses water imagery in the traditional sense — that is, to suggest the life source itself and the transition of the life cycle from one phase to another.

Water imagery also depicts the theme of rebirth, regeneration, and purification, which Bradbury also uses throughout his writings. He incorporates the rebirth image into his "celebrate life" theme. Bradbury urges us to enjoy being alive in spite of life's difficulties, rather than finding life drudgery because of its difficulties.

Bradbury has high hopes for the future of man and man's acquisition of the most fulfilling life possible (a utopia). He shows his readers a utopian world that can result if they heed his advice, and he describes the horrors that can ensue if certain contemporary tendencies (for example, greed, dependence upon technology, governmental control) aren't stopped. Bradbury always suggests that Earth can be the best possible of all worlds, and he also suggests that humankind, when it has come to grips with itself, can make the world a place in which we can all be as free and as happy as we have ever dreamed.

STUDY HELP

Full Glossary for *Fahrenheit 451*

All's well that is well in the end a paraphrase of Shakespeare's *All's Well That Ends Well*, Act IV, Scene iv, Line 35.

And on either side of the river was there a tree of life, which bore twelve manner of fruits, and yielded her fruit every month; and the leaves of the tree are for the healing of the nations a prophecy from verse two of Revelation 22, the last book in the Bible.

atom-bomb mushroom on August 6, 1945, over Hiroshima, Japan, American pilots dropped the first atomic bomb used in the war. The explosion, which rose in a straight column two hundred miles high, ballooned outward like a huge mushroom.

automatic reflex Beatty uses this term to describe how people stopped using their brains and began depending on nerve functions that require no thought.

Beatty the fire captain, who "baits" Montag, is well-named.

Benjamin Franklin founder of America's first fire company in Boston in 1736.

black beetle-colored helmet in literature, the beetle, with its prominent black horns, is a symbol for Satan. Here, vehicles resemble beetles in the dystopian society.

black cobra the "suction snake" that pumps Mildred's stomach repeats the earlier image of the python; the impersonal handymen who operate it have "eyes of puff adders." The fact that it has an eye suggests a sinister and invasive fiber optic tube that examines the inside of the body's organs and even the soul.

The Book of Job Faber selects this book of the Old Testament, which describes how Job is tested by God. The upshot of Job's struggle with suffering, loss, and temptation is that he learns to trust.

Burning Bright the heading derives from "The Tyger," a poem by William Blake.

cacophony harsh, jarring sound; mindless noise.

Caesar's praetorian guard a reference to the bodyguards that surrounded the Roman Caesars, beginning with Rome's first emperor, Octavian, later named Augustus. While holding back the mob, the praetorians wielded supreme control over the rulers who they sought to protect, and they are thought to have assassinated Caligula and replaced him with Claudius, a crippled historian who was their choice of successor.

Carcasses bleed at the sight of the murderer a line from Robert Burton's *Anatomy of Melancholy*, Part I, Section I, Member 2, Subsection 5.

centrifuge the sight of being spun in a great gyre delineates Montag's impression of separation from reality.

Cheshire cat a grinning cat, a character from Chapter 6 of Lewis Carroll's *Alice in Wonderland*.

Clarisse the girl's name derives from the Latin word for *brightest*.

coat of a thousand colors Granger alludes to Joseph, the character in Genesis 37:3-4 who receives a long-sleeved, ornamental coat of many colors from Jacob, his doting father. The coat, symbolizing favoritism shown by Jacob toward his son, alienates the other sons, who sell their brother to passing traders, stain the coat with goat's blood, and return it to their father to prove that a wild animal has eaten Joseph.

Consider the lilies of the field. They toil not, neither do they In his surreal dash on the subway toward Faber's house, Montag tries to read a line from Jesus' Sermon on the Mount from the Gospel of St. Matthew. The line, which is taken from Chapter 6, verses 28-29, concludes, "And yet I say unto you, that even Solomon in all his glory was not arrayed like one of these." This quotation reminds Montag that spiritual hunger is greater than material need.

cricket English slang for fair play; sportsmanship.

crying in the wilderness Granger compares his group's minority status to John the Baptist, the prophet whom Isaiah predicted would one day announce the coming of the Messiah (Isaiah 40: 3-5).

dentrifice any preparation for cleaning teeth. This word is part of the phrase that Montag hears repeatedly in the subway.

The Devil can cite Scripture for his purpose from Shakespeare's *Merchant of Venice*, Act I, Scene iii, Line 99.

The dignity of truth is lost with much protesting a line from Ben Jonson's *Catiline's Conspiracy*, Act III, Scene ii.

A dwarf on a giant's shoulders sees the furthest of the two from *Democritus to the Reader*, Robert Burton's paraphrase from Lucan's *Civil War*, which is echoed in Sir Isaac Newton's letter to Robert Hooke, February 5, 1675 or 1676.

electronic bees futuristic "seashell ear-thimbles" that block out thoughts and supplant them with mindless entertainment.

Faber the character's name suggests that of Peter Faber (1506-1545), tutor of Ignatius Loyola and founder of two Jesuit colleges.

fire plus water Montag, who perceives the split halves of his being, anticipates the distillation of his fiery self into wine after Faber has molded his intellect with wisdom and teaching.

The folly of mistaking a metaphor for a proof, a torrent of verbiage for a spring of capital truths, and oneself as an oracle is inborn in us a paraphrase of Paul Valery's *Introduction to the Method of Leonardo da Vinci.*

451 degrees Fahrenheit the temperature at which book paper catches fire and burns.

the guild of the asbestos-weaver Montag associates his desire to stop the burning with the formation of a new trade union. Like the guilds of the Middle Ages, the asbestos-weavers symbolize progress against the tyranny of the past.

Guy Montag his name suggests two significant possibilities — Guy Fawkes, the instigator of a plot to blow up the English Houses of Parliament in 1605, and Montag, a trademark of Mead, an American paper company, which makes stationery and furnaces.

half out of the cave Bradbury alludes to Plato's cave allegory, found in Book 7 of his *Republic*. The analogy describes how people rely on flickering shadows as their source of reality.

He is no wise man that will quit a certainty for an uncertainty an aphorism from Dr. Samuel Johnson's *Idler.*

I hate a Roman named Status Quo! Granger's grandfather made a pun out of the Latin phrase, which means the situation as it now exists.

Icarus the son of Daedalus; escaping from Crete by flying with wings made of Daedalus, Icarus flies so high that the sun's heat melts the wax by which his wings are fastened, and he falls to his death in the sea. Beatty alludes to Icarus with the comment: "Old Montag wanted to fly near the sun and now that he's burnt his damn wings, he wonders why."

In again out again Finnegan a common nonsense rhyme indicating Mrs. Phelps' lack of concern about the war and her husband's part in it. The quotation restates "Off again, on again, gone again, Finnegan," a terse telegram about a rail crash from Finnegan (a railroad boss) to Flanagan (his employer).

infinitely lacking limits or bounds; extending beyond measure or comprehension.

It is computed that eleven thousand persons have at several times suffered death rather than submit to break their eggs at the smaller end Jonathan Swift illustrates the pettiness of human controversy in Book I, Chapter 4 of *Gulliver's Travels*. The satire found in Swift's writing emphasizes the absurd extent to which society will go to enforce conformity. When Montag reads this quote to Millie, he is pointing out that people are willing to die rather than conform, even though others may believe their position to be absurd or irrational.

Keystone Comedy from 1914 to 1920, director Mack Sennett and Keystone Studios produced a series of madcap silent film comedies featuring the Keystone Cops.

A kind of excellent dumb discourse a line from Shakespeare's *Tempest*, Act III, Scene iii, Line 38.

Knowledge is more than equivalent to force an aphorism from Chapter 13 of Dr. Samuel Johnson's *Rasselas*.

Knowledge is power a line from Francis Bacon's *Advancement of Learning*, Book I, i, 3.

A little learning is a dangerous thing. Drink deep, or taste not the Pierian spring; There shallow draughts intoxicate the brain, and drinking largely sobers us again a famous pair of couplets from Alexander Pope's *Essay on Criticism*, which warns the learner that scholarship requires dedication for maximum effect.

man in the moon the perception of children that the contours of the moon's surface are a face, which peers down at them. The image reflects the oppressive nature of a society that burns books because the man in the moon is always watching them.

mausoleum a large, imposing tomb; often a symbol of death used in literature. Used to describe the interior of Guy's bedroom.

moonstones an opal, or a milky-white feldspar with a pearly luster, used as a gem. The moonstone is connected with Mercury, the mythological guide who leads souls to the underworld.

morphine or procaine a sedative and an anesthetic.

Mr. Jefferson? Mr. Thoreau? Thomas Jefferson, the chief author of the Declaration of Independence, and Henry David Thoreau, author of *Walden* and *Civil Disobedience*. This phrase is used to illustrate that all books and authors are valuable. These two authors are chosen to show who wrote about revolution and fighting opression.

November 4 the firemen play cards early on Mischief Day (November 4), the eve of Guy Fawkes Day, when bonfires and burning of guys in effigy commemorate his Gunpowder Plot, an abortive attempt to destroy James I and his Protestant supporters, who oppressed Catholics.

Oh God, he speaks only of his horse a paraphrase of "he doth nothing but talk of his horse" from Shakespeare's *Merchant of Venice*, Act I, Scene ii, Lines 37-38.

our fingers in the dike an allusion to the legend about the Dutch boy who performed a noble, selfless public service in holding back the sea by keeping his finger in a hole in the dike.

phoenix in Egyptian mythology, a lone bird that lives in the Arabian desert for 500 or 600 years and then sets itself on fire, rising renewed from the ashes to start another long life; a symbol of immortality.

pigeon-winged books the books come alive and flap their "wings" as they are thrown into the fire. This connection between books and birds continues throughout the text and symbolizes enlightenment through reading.

Play the man, Master Ridley; we shall this day light such a candle, by God's grace, in England, as I trust shall never be put out! Bishops Hugh Latimer and Nicholas Ridley, Protestant supporters of the late Queen Jane Grey, were burned at the stake for heresy at Oxford on October 16, 1555. They refused to endorse Queen Mary, a Catholic, claiming that she was an illegitimate daughter of Henry VIII, born after he married his late brother's wife, Catherine of Aragon. Later, Captain Beatty recites the latter portion of the quotation and indicates that he knows something of history.

pratfall slang for a fall on the buttocks, especially one for comic effect, as in burlesque.

proboscis a tubular organ for sensing; nose or snout.

salamander a mythological reptile, resembling a lizard, that was said to live in fire. In the concept of nature, the salamander is a visual representation of fire. In mythology, it endures the flames without burning.

the salamander devours its tail Faber, who creates a way to implicate firemen in their own menace and therefore eradicate them, characterizes his plot with an image of self-destruction.

the sheep returns to the fold. We're all sheep who have strayed at times Beatty alludes to the prophecy in Isaiah 53:6: "All we like sheep have gone astray; we have turned ever one to his own way; and the Lord hath laid on him the iniquity of us all." The message implies that Montag has betrayed his fellow firemen.

Stoneman and Black firemen whose names suggest that the hardness of their hearts and the color of their skin and hair come from contact with smoke.

Sweet food of sweetly uttered knowledge a line from Sir Philip Sidney's *Defense of Poesy*.

That favorite subject. Myself. taken from a letter of the British biographer James Boswell, dated July 16, 1763. The quotation emphasizes the chasm that separates Montag from Mildred, who shuns self-analysis and submerges herself in drugs and the television programs that sedate her mind.

That's what the lady said snappy stage comeback that Mildred uses in place of normal conversation.

There is no terror, Cassius, in your threats, for I am arm'd so strong in honesty that they pass by me as an idle wind, which I respect not Beattytaunts Montag with a passage from Shakespeare's *Julius Caesar*, Act IV, Scene iii, Line 66.

theremin named after Russian inventor Leon Theremin; an early electronic musical instrument whose tone and loudness are controlled by moving the hands in the air between two projecting antennas.

there's lots of old Harvard degrees on the tracks Faber refers to the educated people who have dropped out of sight to live the hobo life outside the city.

They are never alone that are accompanied with noble thoughts a verse taken from Sir Philip Sidney's *Arcadia*, which in turn paraphrases a line from Beaumont and Fletcher's *Love's Cure*, Act III, Scene iii.

This age thinks better of a gilded fool, than of a threadbare saint in wisdom's school a couplet from Thomas Dekker's *Old Fortunatus*.

this electronic cowardice Faber, an old man who is too fearful to confront Captain Beatty, is willing to direct Montag's confrontation through his electronic listening and speaking device.

this great python the fire hose, which resembles a great serpent; a key image in the novel that serves as a reminder of Adam and Eve's temptation to disobey God in the Garden of Eden.

Time has fallen asleep in the afternoon sunshine from Chapter 1 of *Dreamthorp*, a collection of essays by Alexander Smith, a Glasgow lacemaker.

To everything there is a season Montag recalls an often-quoted segment of Ecclesiastes 3:1-8, which reminds him that there is a time for dying as well as a time for living.

Tower of Babel in Genesis 11:1-9, the mythic explanation of how Noah's children came to speak different languages. The word *babel* means a confusion of voices, languages, or sounds.

trench mouth an infectious disease characterized by ulceration of the mucous membranes of the mouth and throat and caused by a bacterium; derived from its prevalence among soldiers in trenches.

Truth is truth, to the end of reckoning Beatty's montage of quotations rambles on to a verse from Shakespeare's *Measure for Measure*, Act V, Scene i, Line 45.

Truth will come to light, murder will not be hid long! from Shakespeare's *Merchant of Venice*, Act II, Scene ii, Line 86.

TV parlor a multidimensional media family that draws the viewer into action, thereby supplanting the viewer's real family.

the tyranny of the majority from John Emerich Edward Dalberg-Acton's *History of Freedom and Other Essays.*

V-2 rocket the German's use of the first long-range, liquid-fuel missile carrying a ton of explosives during World War II changed the face of modern warfare.

Vesuvius a volcano near Naples that erupted August 24, 79 A.D., burying the citizens of Pompeii and Herculaneum.

We cannot tell the precise moment when friendship is formed. As in filling a vessel drop by drop, there is at last a drop which makes it run over; so in a series of kindnesses there is at last one which makes the heart run over from James Boswell's *Life of Dr. Johnson*, published in 1791. The quotation helps Montag understand his relationship with the mysterious Clarisse, who brings joy into his life for no obvious reason.

whisper of a scythe an extended metaphor begins with a giant hand sowing the grains of bombs over the land. The image concludes with the death-dealing scythe, the symbol carried in the hand of Father Time, an image of death, which cuts down life in a single, silent sweep.

Who are a little wise, the best fools be a line from John Donne's poem "The Triple Fool," which Beatty uses to confuse and stifle Montag.

Words are like leaves and where they most abound, Much fruit of sense beneath is rarely found Beatty quotes a couplet from Alexander Pope's *Essay on Criticism* as cynical commentary on his profusely garbled and contradictory recitation.

You think you can walk on water Beatty alludes to Jesus walking on water, as recorded in Mark 6:45-51.

Essay Questions

1. Trace the steps that lead to Montag's decision to preserve books rather than destroy them.

2. Discuss the idea of conformity versus individuality as presented in *Fahrenheit 451*.

3. Choose one important character in the novel and write a character analysis that includes appearance, actions, ideas, manner, reactions of others to the character, and feelings of the character throughout the novel. Do the character's feelings or ideals change? Why is this character important to the novel? How well does this character fit into a utopian and dystopian society?

4. Compare and contrast the characters of Mildred and Clarisse. How is one a threat to the stability of the ideas presented in *Fahrenheit 451* and the other an ideal example of a *Fahrenheit 451* character? How have each of these characters been influenced?

5. What roles do Clarisse, the Unidentified Old Woman, Faber, and Beatty play in reeducating Guy Montag? How does each character influence Montag's change? How do these characters question his beliefs? How does he answer their questions?

6. Explain how the titles to the three parts of the book are significant to the general action that occurs within each part.

7. What messages or themes is Ray Bradbury trying to impart on his audience? What things in society is he commenting on? Could this type of society really exist? Why or why not?

8. In comparing and contrasting the film and book of *Fahrenheit 451*, point out three similarities and three differences between the book and film. Then explain why, you believe, changes were made in the film.

9. Write an essay detailing the ideological issues involved in censorship.

10. Discuss the dual image of fire in the novel.

11. Examine the psychological complexity of Captain Beatty. Account for his knowledge of books, while also accounting for his desire to burn them.

12. Explain why no female characters are alive at the end of the novel. Why did both female characters die in the novel, but in the film, why does Clarisse, as a human book living in the woods, survive and greet Montag?

Practice Projects

1. Design your own Web site about *Fahrenheit 451* and describe what content would be featured on the pages of your Web site.

2. Design a poster illustrating a scene from the novel or capturing a theme in the novel.

3. Become the director of the film version of *Fahrenheit 451*. Who would you cast? What would you change about the movie, and what would you definitely keep? Design your movie trailer: What scenes would you include? Choose music that you would use for important scenes.

4. Interview a character from *Fahrenheit 451*. Write at least ten questions that will give the character the opportunity to discuss his thoughts and feelings about his role in the novel. Choose an interview style that you would want to present this interview.

5. Write a journal that one of the *Fahrenheit 451* main characters may have kept before, during, and after the book's events.

6. Write a newspaper story about what happened at the end or during a part of *Fahrenheit 451*. Include photos of the action.

7. Find a song or poem or several songs and poems that relate to themes presented in *Fahrenheit 451*. Write out the lyrics/words and then explain how they relate to *Fahrenheit 451*.

8. Write a paper on the literature of dystopian fiction and explain how *Fahrenheit 451* partakes of this tradition.

Quiz

1. Faber a former professor of which subject?
A) English
B) History
C) Law
D) Mathematics

2. In what century does the story take place?
A) 21st
B) 22nd
C) 24th
D) 29th

3. What is Captain Beatty's relationship with books?
A) He doesn't know how to read and is ashamed of it.
B) He hates books vehemently and is proud he has never read one.
C) He is well read but enforces the state views about books.
D) He thinks they are a good form of entertainment if not taken too seriously.

4. What is the imposing threat throughout this novel?
A) Alien invasion
B) Natural disasters
C) Nuclear meltdown
D) War

5. What is the primary duty of the firemen in the novel?
A) To burn illegal books
B) To burn people who defy laws
C) To fight fires
D) To protect free speech

6. What poem does Montag read to his wife, Mrs. Phelps, and Mrs. Bowles?
A) Dover Beach
B) Leda and the Swan
C) Ode on a Grecian Urn
D) Ulysses

7. Which character says the following: □Play the man, Master Ridley; we shall this day light such a candle, by God's grace, in England, as I trust shall never be put out.□

A) Captain Beatty
B) Clarisse
C) Mildred
D) The old woman

8. Which of the following is a highly motivating force of change for Montag?

A) Admonishment by Beatty
B) Millie's suicide attempt
C) The Mechanical Hound's growling
D) The old woman's death

9. Who is the leader of the social outcasts and criminals?

A) Black
B) Clara Phelps
C) Granger
D) Stoneman

10. Who says the following: □Give a man a few lines of verse and he thinks he's the Lord of all Creation. You think you can walk on water with your books.□

A) Captain Beatty
B) Faber
C) Granger
D) Guy Montag

11. Why is Clarisse unique?

A) She goes to school.
B) She goes to therapy.
C) She likes conversation.
D) She loves the TV family.

Answers: 1.A 2.C 3.C 4.D 5.A 6.A 7.D 8.D 9.C 10.A 11.C

NOTES

NOTES

Made in the USA
Las Vegas, NV
12 January 2026

39168310R00049